GMC II

GET MONEY CLIQUE

JAMES A. NEAL

CONTENTS

ACKNOWLEDGEMENTS

THIS RIGHT HERE WAS THE HARDEST PART OF WRITING this book because there are so many people to thank and so many people who have influenced me in life and shown me so much love. First and foremost, let me start off by thanking my city St. Petersburg, for standing 100% behind me. Trust me, I would not have done it without y'all. I love my city! I cannot forget about the rest of the people from different states who showed me love as well by supporting my first book, GMC Get Money Clique. Now that GMC 2 is out, let us run it back up, yeah that part. Can't stop won't stop. Shout out to both of my beautiful daughters, Karmella Neal and Janyla Neal, y'all are the ones that keep me motivated in life to achieve all my goals. I would like to say rest in peace to both of my parents, James Allen Neal and Annie Doris Neal. I did it again! Y'all told me that I was a rising star, that all I had to do is trust in God. To put my mind to it and that I can be whatever I want to. Wow, who knew that I will be an Author. God is good for giving me the talent to do what I truly love, writing books. Big shout out to my best friend, my wife, my business partner, my heart, Nancy Neal; the CEO/Manager of Street Dreams Publishing.

Thank you for your help building up this company and making it what it is today. Shout out to LuBGYNOT and Street Dreams ENT. We are going all the way to the top. Shout out to my brothers and sisters Tushawn Coleman, Stephanie Neal, Tangela Oliver, Nina Lang, Denoca Oliver, Curtis Lang and Oran walker. Shout out to all my nieces, nephews and cousins, I love you all. Shout out to my hood, 21st street and Queensboro. We did it again, put one in the air. To all my Real Rights, y'all know who you are. ILMB! Free all my Real Right Billys. B.I.P to the Big Billy, Garland "S.I." Tyree. B.I.P Baby red and to the rest of the fallen soldiers that we lost throughout the years. R.I.P to my Uncle Craig. R.I.P Uncle Ernest Harris. I cannot forget about my little homie Sebastian LLBash A.K.A Mr. 21st. It hurts me a lot that you are not here anymore. The last time we talked I told you that I will be releasing the second book. I cannot question god, but I know you are in a better place. You will forever be missed by family and friends, 21st for Life. Another hood banger is out, and success does not come over night. You have to put in work and go get what is yours.

PROLOGUE

NITRO WAS HOME SITTING ON THE COUCH WATCHING A gangster movie called "King of New York" when he heard his phone ring. He looked at his phone screen to see who it was and answered the call. "What's up Bae?" He repeated himself as he couldn't hear the caller. He then grabbed his remote to turn down the volume on the television. To his surprise, he heard Eisha's voice.

"Listen Angie, she was in the way of me and Nitro, so I killed that Bitch. She had to be stopped." Nitro's jaw dropped when he heard those words come out of Eisha's mouth. He could not believe she was the one who killed Brenda. "Angie, I don't give a fuck how he felt about that bitch. Now we can finally start a family," she said laughing in the background as Nitro listened.

"Girl you crazy for real," Angie said getting up to fix herself a strong drink. "You good, you want anything to drink?" Angie asked as she headed towards the bar. "Nawl, I'm okay but I am going to call the babysitter and check up on my baby," Eisha replied as she pulled out her phone. Just as she began to dial out, her phone lit up.

"WHAT THE FUCK!" thought Eisha. Her eyes grew bigger as she read the display on her phone. She noticed the call time and her heart dropped when she saw Nitro's name.

"FUCK!" Eisha bawled out.

CHAPTER 1: NITRO'S SURPRISE

NITRO RUSHED INTO HIS WALK-IN CLOSET TO GRAB some money from a shoe box when he noticed some things out of place. He grabbed his red shoe box from deep off in the corner, looked inside and noticed Brenda's diamond necklace and DVD that he bought for her. Nitro grabbed the disc and popped it inside his DVD player; curious to see what was on it. To his surprise, he saw himself pounding Eisha and instantly thought how Eisha was a dirty bitch.

CHAPTER 2: THE GETAWAY

"**L**ISTEN ANGIE, YOU CAN'T TELL NITRO WHERE I AM." Eisha said nervously.

"Where do you plan on going?" Angie asked.

"I don't know but I have to get my baby and get the fuck out of town," Eisha replied, grabbing her car keys.

"Damn Eisha, do you really think that was Nitro?" Angie asked. "Yes Angie, he heard the whole fucking conversation. I can't go back to the house. Nitro will kill me. I will call you as soon as I touch down, now let me go get my baby." Eisha gave her friend one last hug before rushing out the door, jumping into her car, and taking off.

One hour later Eisha was at St. Pete-Clearwater Airport waiting on the next flight to ATL. She viewed the time on the check list board and then looked at her watch that read 4:30pm. Eisha noticed that she was on time for the next flight to Atlanta. She then grabbed her baby's car seat, with the baby inside and rushed through the crowded airport. She instantly stopped in her tracks when she saw Nitro and Big Joe standing by the flight of stairs where you enter to board the plane. She almost shitted in her underwear as Nitro walked up to her and peacefully said, "So where do you think you're going?" He put his arm around her neck, walking her towards a black-on-black SUV. Big Joe was standing with the back door open.

"Nitro please, I am sorry," she said with a pleading look in her eyes. Big Joe helped Eisha get into the back seat with her baby. Eisha was a bit frightened because Nitro didn't say one word to her and she didn't know what his next move would be.

"How can you explain this," Nitro said pushing the play button on the remote. Eisha's heart dropped to the bottom of her stomach, when she noticed Nitro had found the DVD she made with the two of them having sex.

"Nitro, I am sorry," she said. "Sorry is not going to cut it. How you do some shit like that," he yelled. I trusted you and you betrayed me." Eisha was sitting on the couch crying with her face buried into her palms.

"Nitro, please, I am sorry for what I did but I love you the same way she did," She said with her eyes watery and nose running.

"Eisha, did you know when you killed Brenda you took away my unborn child as well," Nitro yelled out.

Eisha did not know Brenda was pregnant, Nitro kept it a secret. The only person Nitro told was trouble. He planned on wait a good time to tell his clique about his precious gift. Eisha was devastated to hear the news.

At the time, Eisha felt like she wanted to roll over and die because she realized that she took a child's life. She felt like a cold-blooded killer. Nitro and Eisha continue to go back and forth with words.

CHAPTER 3: HERE COMES TROUBLE

TAMEKA WAS ON HER KNEES IN HER BATHROOM throwing up inside her toilet after just leaving a horrible crime scene. She just witnessed a family of four with gunshot wounds, each to the head, execution style. She never seen anything like that and it hit her hard to see two kids, ages four and five, lose their life at such a young age. Tameka looked down at her cellphone as she seen it vibrating on the bathroom floor. Bzzzzzzzzzz...Bzzzzzzzzzz...Bzzzzzzzzzz, she picked it up and saw three text messages. She pressed the inbox button and read Troubles last text... Call me.

Trouble was riding up the block nodding his head to the sound of Soulja Slim & BG blasting out his speakers while he puffed on some Purp. Trouble felt his cellphone go off vibrating in his lap Bzzzzzz... Bzzzzzzzzzz... Bzzzzzzzzzz.. He quickly turned down his music and answered the call. "What's up Bae?"

"Hey!" Tameka replied as she rubbed her smooth legs down with some Coco Butter lotion. "What's wrong Bae? Are you just getting up or something?"

"Oh no, I just had a long day at work and I just wanted to come home and relax."

"I know what you need Ma, a good massage." Trouble said.

"Is that right, I know how your massages can be," she said with a grin on her face.

"So, if you know, then you know the boss don't mind coming over putting in work," he replied as he inhaled the weed smoke.

"I don't have a problem with the boss coming over. Just let the boss know that I love putting in over time," she said pulling out a set of lingerie from her dresser.

"Okay, I'll be there in 20 minutes."

"Alright, hurry, the boss doesn't want to keep Ms. Kitty waiting. You know how she can get when she has to wait," Tameka said in a sexy tone as she bit down on her bottom lip.

Trouble felt his dick raising every minute he chatted with her on the phone. Trouble didn't waste no time, he was in front of Tameka's house in less than twenty minutes, knocking on the door. Tameka answered the door with a brown towel wrapped around her head wearing a white robe. Trouble could easily tell that she just got out of the shower, so he knew that pussy was going to be good and wet.

"Wow, that was quick," she said with a smile.

"You know I can't have my Kitty waiting too long," Trouble replied stepping inside, taking a seat on the couch while Tameka walked into the kitchen and started pouring two glasses of red wine. Trouble had sat back and continued to think about his plot on how he could flood the prisons with the deadly poison. When he looked up, Tameka was coming toward him wearing a lace bra and thong, with two glasses of wine in her hand. She handed Trouble his drink and told him to sit back and enjoy, while she went to work. Trouble never had his dick sucked by Tameka before, so he couldn't wait to see what her head game was like.

Tameka took one more sip of her drink before she sat it down, then squatted between his legs. Trouble looked down at her as she reached in his sweat pants and pulled out his dick. "Ima do what you tell me, baby," she grinned as she ran the tip of her tongue around the rim of his dick. Trouble held eye contact with her as she began to suck gently on the head, bringing him to attention. When he looked down, her pretty pussy was staring back at him and his shit went from rock to brick. Tameka Squeezed tightly at the base, moving her wrist enough to bring him in and out of her mouth. She was getting it sloppy wet with every motion; tightening her grip and her jaws while rolling her tongue back and forth over that main vein.

"Whoooooooo..." he breathed deeply as his left hand gripped the arm of the couch. "Mmmmm..." She moaned, taking in all of him. Releasing him from her jaws, she stroked him quick and firmly while sensually rolling her tongue up and down his length making full eye contact. When she heard another deep breath leave his lips, she took him in her mouth and all the way to the back of her throat. Gripping each hand on his knees, she titled his dick forward and gave him that no hands action. The faster and harder she sucked the heavier he breathed. "Damn, Ma," he mumbled as the intensity of her wet treat brought him to the edge of no return.

"Mmmmm..." She moaned, causing the right amount of vibration. Removing her hands from his knees, she grabbed him with one hand and gently caressed his balls with the other. Rotating her wrist, sucking and caressing him with her mouth brought it on. Trouble dug his fingertips into the couch as he released. Tameka allowed a little to enter her mouth and then rundown the length of his dick. She then ran the tip of her Tongue down the back and up and down the line between his sac, playing in his essence.

"I love you," she whispered, rising from between his legs.

Slightly dazed and satisfied, he moaned, "I love you too. I am going to give you a bonus for the good work you put in," Trouble said with a grin on his face.

"I just wanted to let you know that you're in charge." She bit down on her bottom lip, giving him her fuck me gaze.

"Is that right?" he stood up towering over her, he sized up the situation, realizing he needed to return the favor.

"If I'm in charge, where do you think you need to be positioned at?" he asked pulling his shirt over his head and throwing it to the floor. "Right by your side," she cooed.

"That's what I like to hear," he said scooping her up and placing her pussy at mouth level.

Tameka draped her legs over his shoulders and rubbed his head as he walked to the living room wall, placing her back firmly against it. Then his tongue made the first contact with her clit, and she put her head back on the wall and allowed him to worship her, thinking this is the man she wanted to spend the rest of her life with. Tameka continued to paint his lips with her honey.

CHAPTER 4: PARANOIA

EISHA WAS HOME TAKING A HOT SHOWER TRYING TO ease her mind. Paranoid at the same time because Nitro told her that he will be keeping his kid for a couple of days until he calls her and let her know when she can come and pick him up. Eisha slid the shower curtain back and noticed her gun was gone. She then grabbed a towel to wrap around her body. Eisha knew that she wasn't bugging out, so she checked her other stash spot underneath the bathroom sink, but that gun was removed as well. Eisha became nervous and eased out the bathroom door quietly creeping down the hallway.

Eisha knew someone was in her house because her living room and kitchen lights were turned off. She then heard shattering glass, making her turn around quickly. A black shadow shot off the hallway wall making Eisha look in the opposite way. She then took off running towards the front door where she did not make it. Psst...Psst...Psss... Psst...Psss the 9mm with the silencer dropped her right where she stood.

It was 12:30am. Nitro was getting ready to head out the door when he got a call letting him know that the job was done. An hour later, he pulled up in front of club Scene. There were two long lines extending the length of the long city block, one for women and one for men. Nitro exiting his ride, exchanged hugs and pounds with the valet before handing over his keys. Nitro was famous for urban fashion; Polo down with the brown & black buckle and shell toe Polo boots to match. He was known for staying fresh in all types of gear. Timberlands, sneakers, jeans, sweat suits and any other garments or accessories made popular by the latest hip hop artists. A big, dark skin, muscle bound bouncer with a shiny bald head greeted him, ushering him inside as if he was an artist set to perform. A song by TI flowed throughout the club as Nitro took in the scenery. He spotted the club owner Rick coming his way and they exchanged a few words while heading to the VIP section. Rick was a short, slim built white boy, whose parents had mad cake. He owned several night clubs in Tampa and St. Pete. Trouble wanted to rob Rick, but Nitro stopped him from doing so because Rick's grandma went to the same church as his and he knew that he could ask Rick for anything and he would not have a problem giving it to him.

"Damn my brother it's been a while since we last talked. What brought you out tonight?" Rick asked with two diamond chains around his neck.

"I had to get out and clear my mind a little," Nitro replied splitting a cigar open and dumping the inside guts. "What's the problem? Because you know we got money to take care of any problem that comes our way or act like it's coming our way," Rick stated taking a sip from his glass.

"Oh no fam, everything's cool. The problem was already taken care of" Nitro said breaking up sticky weed inside the gar. He never thought in a lifetime that he would have to kill Eisha but that's how the game goes. Nitro took everything to the heart. How Eisha betrayed him by killing Brenda and their unborn child, now he must raise his son without his son's mother being around. He knows it will be a tough job, but his son will understand once he gets older.

"So how everything been going? I hear you are doing big things," Rick said passing Nitro a lighter to fire up the blunt.

"You know I am just trying to get my cake like everyone else. But on some real getting money shit, you're the one who's doing big things,

Mr. Partnership, CIROC owner with Diddy. Yeah, you thought I didn't know" Nitro said with a laugh before inhaling the weed smoke.

"Yeah fam, I am getting serious paper now. At first, he didn't want to fuck with me but when he started to see me land in helicopters and pushing Lambos, he got his mind right and started to fuck with the kid."

"Oh, I already know you showed him all of your toys. That nigga must think he the only one with money." Nitro said, taking one last hit of the blunt before passing it to Rick.

"Excuse me Rick but a brother like me got a sweet tooth and a taste for chocolate. As a matter of fact, I see a nice little chocolate bunny I wanna get to know." Rick's eyes followed Nitro's.

"Yeah, she bad," Rick said.

'That's the truth," Nitro replied. The thick woman in stiletto heels and a mini skirt sat two couches down. "Pardon me, Rick. That young lady is hungry, and I got all the meat she needs." With that, he walked over and sat beside the woman, getting a closeup of them full lips and round eyes. She was sipping a margarita.

CHAPTER 5: MS. LADY

"**E**XCUSE ME, MISS. I DON'T MEAN TO INVADE YOUR space, but I like what I see and when I see something I like, I go for it."

"People around here call me Nitro and yours," he said with his hand extended out.

"Ashley, she replied, shaking his hand as she crossed her thick thighs.

"So, you like what you see?" she said, seductively gazing into Nitro's eyes. His pupils veered down between her legs, then back to her eyes.

"I want what I see."

"Sometimes people bite off more than they can chew" Ashley stated.

"Listen baby," Nitro eased his arm between himself and the woman looking at his Rolex.

"Every minute I waste, I'm losing money and getting older. Were both adults, so let's skip the preliminaries and get to the main event." He stood and held his hand out when the woman grabbed it. Nitro helped her from the couch and they both exited the club. One hour later, Ashley watched as Nitro clumsily stumbled onto the motel bed.

He gripped his rock-hard dick and Ashley almost felt sorry for him. She knew that Lambo would kill him as he was ordered to do. Ashley walked over to Nitro and dropped to her knees. She then began to unbutton his Polo jeans and pull out his dick.

"Just relax Nitro, let me take care of you," she said as she took Nitro's ten inches into her mouth. She purposely left the door unlocked so Lambo could creep in and kill Nitro. Where this Nigga at? He's taking all day, she thought as she continued to go up and down on Nitro's shaft then began playing with the tip of it with her tongue. She paused to look at Nitro and as she looked up, what she saw scared the living shit out of her. No longer looking distraught and confused like he was moments before. Nitro was smiling with his pistol in his hand. His demeanor totally changed. Nitro played like he was wasted, he already peeped game when she shot out the text letting whoever she was texting, know that the door would be unlocked.

"You look surprised," Nitro said just before he struck her in the temple causing her to fly onto the carpeted floor.

She gripped her bloody forehead in agony and her vision became temporarily blurred.

"You thought I didn't see you send that text? Huh? I ain't new to this, I'm true to this!" Nitro yelled as he stood up and put his dick back in his jeans.

"Now look at you!" he said, his gun pointed at Ashley.

"That's why Niggas can't trust you hoes out here! I know a Nigga is about to come in here any second now. I saw your dumb ass leave the door unlocked and I peeped you talking to that Nigga who was in that blue car that followed us here."

"Nitro, wait I—"

Nitro struck her again in the head with the butt of the gun. Then he aimed the gun at her head once again. "Who sent you," Nitro asked ready to squeeze down on the trigger.

"Miko, sent mm____," before Ashley could get out her sentence, Nitro sent a hollow tip through her skull with his silenced pistol.

All he needed to hear was a name now his only concern was the guy who was scheduled to come in the room at any second.

CHAPTER 6: COCAINE COWBOYS

TAMEKA WAS LAID UP NEXT TO TROUBLE IN BED WATCHING a documentary of the cocaine cowboys.

"Oh my God, that old lady really killed all them people?"

"Yeah, she did. That's the Black Widow, she didn't play when it came to her money and running things her way," Troubled stated.

"That old lady right there, nobody ain't want to fuck with her back in them days."

Tameka heard a story about the Cocaine Cowboys, she just couldn't believe how an old lady could have so much power.

CHAPTER 7: LAMBO

NITRO STOOD OVER LAMBO'S SHAKING BODY, WATCHING him struggle for life. Nitro caught him with four slugs to the chest, right as he walked through the motel door and held the smoking gun in his hand. Nitro witnessed Lambo take his last breath and then quickly fled the scene.

CHAPTER 8: PACMAN

8:30am

PACMAN WAS RIDING UP 275, GETTING HIS DICK SUCKED by a badass Latina that he met last night in the club. He was on his way to Tallahassee with five bricks stashed inside the middle of his dashboard. He looked in his rearview mirror and noticed the red & blue lights flashing behind him. "Oh shit," he said, telling himself not to panic. The girl raised her head up to see what was going on. She also noticed the flashing lights on the cop car.

"Oh my God, I hope they didn't see me," she said with her right hand covering her mouth.

"Nawl ma, just sit back and relax. Don't say shit I got this." Pacman quickly put his dick back into his pants and then pulled over off to the side of the interstate. He reached under his shirt pulling his Glock 40 from his waistline placing it under his seat. He reached over and stuck his hand inside the girl's purse pulling out a bottle of Chanel fragrance, spraying a large amount in the air trying to kill the weed smell.

Detective White & Detective Green stepped out of their unmarked cruisers. Detective White walked up on the driver side of Pacman's smoke gray, Audi S4 and tapped on the window. Pacman rolled down his window as he stared Detective White right in the eyes.

"Too late for that cowboy," Detective White stated with a smile, smelling the fragrance mix with the heavy Marijuana that was in the air. "How can I help you officer?" Pacman said, with a pleading look in his eyes.

'Yes, you can first help me by stepping out of the car. You and that beautiful girl you're with."

"For what reason officers," Pacman replied, trying to see why he had to step out the car.

"This is not a back & forth question game. Either you step out this mutha fuckin car or I will snatch you out and that will not be a good look," Detective White said, waiting for Pacman to pick his choice. Pacman stepped out of the car with his pants falling to his ankles.

"It looks like someone was getting an early morning wake up," Detective White said, bending down to take a look at the female while she rolled her eyes and looks in the opposite direction. Detective White gave Detective Green a head nod, letting him know to take the girl out the car as well. Detective Green followed suite and asked the girl to step out of the vehicle while Detective White called for a K-9 unit to check the car to see if anything was hidden inside. Detective Green was checking out the gorgeous Latina that was wearing a short jean miniskirt and a shirt that was so tight it looked like an extra layer of skin. Her features were exotic; caramel skin complexion, shiny like a wet candy apple. Detective Green was lost for words to see a girl so beautiful hanging out with a bad guy. On the other hand, Detective White had Pacman in cuffs waiting for the K-9 unite to pull up. What Pacman didn't know was that Detective White was watching every move he made.

"What was inside the brown bag you walked out the house with?" Detective White asked, letting Pacman know that he was being watch.

"Listen dude, I don't know what the hell you're talking about, you have the wrong person," Pacman replied.

"Okay, stand right here and be a nice gentleman," Detective White joked. He then kneeled and began searching the vehicle, flipping everything upside down. Pacman was shitting bricks, hoping he didn't find the burner.

"Aye man, what's up with this shit? You don't even have a fucking warrant to be searching my shit," Pacman bawled out and said with a frown on his face. Detective White came out the car with a hand full of surprises.

'Well, well, well, look what we have here champ. This right here alone will give you ten years max," Detective White said putting everything he found on top of the hood.

"And for your question, yes, I do have a search warrant since I smell marijuana," Detective White said with a smile, knowing that's all he had to say to search anyone's car.

"This is a nice weapon you got here," Detective White said taking the clip out the Glock 40, starting to notice he was working with a full house. Detective Green still had the girl sitting on the sidewalk cuffed with her hands behind her back. He was getting a free peek between her legs when he noticed she wasn't wearing any underwear. He couldn't help but to stare at that smooth shaved cherry. The young lady was giving Detective Green the show of his lifetime. Detective white was checking out some promotional party flyers that had GMC name on it.

"Oh, I remember that event. You know why? Because I was there," Detective White said with a grin. Pacman didn't like the way the Detective was talking to him knowing that he was a dirty cop. Fifteen minutes later a K-9 cruiser pulls up on the scene. Pacman's heart dropped to the bottom of his stomach when he saw the green and white cruiser, he knew that game was over if the dog sniffs out the cocaine.

"So, how about you make this easy on yourself. Let me know what else you have in this car before man's best friend go inside," Detective White said.

"I don't have shit else, you got everything," Pacman replied. A tall, bald headed, redneck stepped out his SUV, letting a brown husky dog Jump out the back seat.

The officer walked up to Detective White and asked "So, what do we have here Detective?" he said giving Detective White a handshake. "Nothing much, just a street punk I been watching for a minute."

Fuck you, pussy ass cracker," Pacman bawled out wishing he had the cuffs off. The tall redneck officer stepped up to Pacman's face, touching nose to nose and said, "Stand there and shut the fuck up before they find your nigger ass hanging from a tree." Detective white sat back to enjoy the show that was taking place.

"Fuck you, pussy ass cracker, you take these cuffs off and I'll beat your ass," Pacman said in an aggressive tone. Detective white stepped up when he noticed the situation was getting out of hand. He grabbed Pacman roughly by the neck, walking him to the car and throwing him into the backseat. Pacman had continued to carry on with the commotion. The K-9 officer patted his dog on the side telling him to go work. The dog jumped inside the car and used his powerful nose to sniff out any narcotics. Detective White and the K-9 officer sat back and watched the dog tear up the inside of the car.

"Woof, woof, woof" the dog barked, scratching his heavy paws on the dashboard getting Detective White and his masters attention. The officer told his K-9 loudly to cease and the dog immediately came to a standstill. Detective White & the K-9 officer both took the dashboard apart like they were working at an auto repair shop. As they took the dashboard off they both noticed five blocks wrapped in gray duct tape.

"Look what we have here," Detective White said as he took the drugs out one by one, placing the blocks inside the same brown bag that Pacman carried out the house.

"Good job boy," The officer told his K-9 as he patted him on his back.

"Thanks a lot officer. I knew that nigger had something in his car," Detective White said. "No problem, Detective, this is what we are here for; to take down the bad guys." "Take her down to the station, I got what we were looking for," Detective white told his partner holding up the brown bag. Both got in their cruiser taking off to the station.

Fifteen minutes later, Detective White had Pacman in the interrogation room sitting at a round brown table. Pacman had his head cocked back looking directly at Detective White. "So, what do you have to tell me? Whose drugs did we find in your ride?" He asked.

Detective White leaned back in his chair with his feet cocked up on the table, waiting for Pacman to answer the question.

"I don't know what the fuck you're talking about, you didn't find shit in my car," Pacman replied with a serious look.

Detective White quickly jumped out of his seat and rushed over to where Pacman was sitting, grabbed him by the neck roughly trying to get him to talk.

"Pussy boy, you real tough while I got these cuffs on," Pacman said with anger in his voice.

"Listen here you little piece of shit, I already know about your little GMC gang and I promise that I will take every one of you down and I'm starting with you first."

'Now I am going to go in this office to grab a couple of photos and hopefully by the time I come back you will tell me what I need to know," patting Pacman on his left shoulder before walking out. As he opened the second interrogation room door, he saw the Latino chick (that got arrested with Pacman) jumping up and down on Detective Green. Both of her ass cheeks were spread apart as Detective Green drilled off inside her. They paused for a second when Detective White walked inside.

"Why didn't you lock the fucking door stupid?" he asked in a low tone of voice trying not to let some of the other officers hear him.

"Where are the photographs?" Detective White asked while staring at the girls round shaped ass. Detective Green pointed his finger at the microwave that were by a small coffee table. Detective White grabbed the brown folder with the pictures inside then shook his head as he stepped back next door with a grin on his face. Slamming the brown folder down in front of Pacman, he noticed two photos of Nitro and Trouble.

"So, you going to give me my man or do we have to play this game."

'Listen dude, I don't know what the fuck your talking about." Pacman didn't take his eyes off the photos that were laid out in front of him knowing that he knew both of them well.

"Okay here me out tough guy. My Partner is in the other room fucking the dog shit out of your girl, so that should tell you right there she already turned against you," Detective White said with a smile. Pacman was lost for words to hear that the girl had already turned state against him after he done told her to keep her mouth shut.

"My advice to you is to make this easy on yourself and tell me who the leaders of GMC are? If you don't then you can go to prison and be somebody's little bitch for the rest of your life or you can walk out of here a free man. It's all on you." Pacman never thought, throughout his whole twenty-six years, he would be in a situation where he had to give up names to keep his freedom. He never told on anybody but now he was breaking the street code. Detective White waited patiently for Pacman to make his choice. Pacman knew that he couldn't do his whole life behind the prison walls. Pacman took a deep breath before pointing his finger at Nitro's picture. Detective White stood by with a grin on his face after scooping up the photos and taking a seat.

"Okay, you got what you wanted to know. Can I get the fuck out of here?" Pacman stood up and said with his face balled up. Detective White looked up at Pacman and said,

"Oh no chump, you still have work to do. You thought I was going to let you go that easy?" Pacman fell back into his chair with no win waiting to see what was next.

CHAPTER 9: THE PIRATE KIDS

NITRO AND TROUBLE WAS ON THE WAY TO THE SUPER 8 Motel to check up on Lady Red and see how she was holding down everything. Lady Red had taken over the Motel when Ace got killed. She was making sure that everything was on point because if she didn't, she knew that she would be laying in the same place as Ace.

"Bra, I got every soldier on the streets looking for this fuck nigga," Trouble said passing the blunt to Nitro.

"That nigga wasn't nowhere in the club last night when I met that hoe. So that shit was already planned," Nitro said referring to the incident he had to take care of.

"Damn, Homie that's what's up that you were on point. You smoked that Bitch like a cigarette."

"Yeah bra, I know. If I wasn't on point, I wouldn't be right here talking to you today," Nitro said passing the blunt to Trouble. "Don't worry big dawg, that pussy nigga going to feel the Pressure, he can't hide forever," Trouble said.

"The Pirate Kids already ran down and clapped one of his Lil' niggas coming out the store." "Word," Nitro said reaching for the blunt. "Hell yeah! Nitro listen, The Pirate Kids are not playing, them Lil' Niggas murking everything we send a hit on."

"That's what's up," Nitro replied feeling a good high. "So, what's up with you and that baby? Y'all spending a lot of time together." Trouble looked at Nitro with a grin on his face.

"Nawl bra she is good people," Trouble replied.

"Nigga she is more than just good people, all that time you been putting in. I know you Trouble, you just can't tell me anything." Trouble burst into laughter.

"Nigga look who talking. Daughter snatching as Nigga."

"Do El Mayo know that the same Nigga he's selling blocks to, is smashing his daughter?" Trouble said as he turned inside the parking lot of the Motel.

"Nawl bra, it's not like that. We just be vibin," Nitro replied with a grin on his face.

"Damn Nigga, you doin a lot of vibin because you been going to see El Mayo a lot lately."

"Nawl bra this on some business shit, I got to go see him tomorrow."

"See that's what I'm talking about, come on big bra lay it down on me."

"Trouble what are you talking about? I told you I haven't done shit with that girl. We're on a business vibe that's all."

"Yeah right, only time will tell," Trouble replied stepping out the car.

CHAPTER 10: THE INFORMANT

TAMEKA WALKED OVER FROM HER DESK TO KNOCK ON Detective Greens door. "Yes, come in" Detective Green said as he was going through some paperwork. Tameka stepped inside the office and then paused for a minute when she saw Trouble's picture on Detective Green's desk laid out in front of him.

"Yes, how can I help you Detective Foster," he asked staring at her features.

"Yes, did anything come back on the prints with the family of four that got murdered two weeks ago? She asked trying to take her eyes off Trouble's picture.

"Yes, they did. All the fingerprints that got dusted, that day, came back as fingerprints of the family."

Tameka became upset because now she doesn't have any leads to the suspect's. "What's that you got right there in front of you," She asked trying to get any type of information about why Trouble's pictures are sitting on his desk.

"Oh, these two guys we have been investigating for a while now for moving illegal drugs. They call themselves GMC. It stands for Get

Money Clique," Detective Green said with a laugh. Tameka thought to herself, too good to be true. She had a slight feeling that Trouble was in the game, but she can't be mad at him because she lied to him about what she does for a living.

"Right now, we have a confidential informant that's in their circle named Pacman, so hopefully this street gang will be off the streets soon," Detective Green said confidently. Tameka fell in love with Trouble so quick she didn't want to lose him. It was only right she tell him what's going on. "Well, thank you. Let me know if anything new comes up," she said turning around getting ready to walk out of Detective Green's office.

"I sure will Detective," he replied, as he pulled his phone out his top right pocket, getting ready to make a call.

Tameka stepped out of his office and then rushed to the woman's restroom. She pulled out her phone and shot Trouble a text message as that would be the safest way to communicate the information.

Trouble was dropping off Nitro at the house when he felt his phone vibrate inside his pocket "Bra hit me up when you get back in town," Trouble said as he reached inside his pocket.

"Fo-Sho," Nitro replied before closing the door. Trouble Pulled out his cellphone and seen a text message from Tameka that read (come by, 911). Trouble seen the 911 behind the text and thought to himself, what can be such an emergency? Trouble grinned when he answered his own question "Damn, she already missing this dick." Trouble took off rushing through traffic like an ambulance.

Fifteen minutes later, Trouble was knocking on Tameka's door. Tameka opened the door wearing some short black tights with the matching sports bra. She just got finished getting a workout in. Both greeted each other with a kiss. Trouble stepped inside taking a seat down on the soft leather couch. Tameka walked over and took a seat next to Trouble.

"So, what's the emergency?" Trouble said with a grin on his face, thinking Tameka just wanted him to come through and lay down the pipe. Tameka looked Trouble directly in his eyes and said, "You have to kill this dude Pacman that's in your circle."

"And for what reason?" Trouble replied, trying to figure out how Tameka knew one of his soldiers.

"Listen Trouble, I already know what you do, you do not promote," She said as she watched Trouble's grin go to a normal facial expression. You're one of the leaders of GMC," she said.

Trouble was lost for words. He wanted to know how Tameka found that out. Trouble was about to explain but was cut off—"Listen Trouble, I have something that I need to tell you. I am a Detective." Trouble was blown to hear those words come out of Tameka's mouth. He had a feeling that Tameka was lying to him about where she worked, he just couldn't point it out. Trouble quickly stood to his feet getting ready to walk out. Tameka grabbed him by his hand, "No wait," she said keeping eye contact with him. "I am sorry, don't leave," she said with a pleading look. "Why did you lie to me," Trouble said in a low tone voice.

"The same reason you lied to me. I fell in love with you. I don't care about my job or none of that bullshit, the reason why I didn't tell you when we first met was because I thought you would have looked at me differently. I am not here to take you down or set you up, I fell in love with you and I hope you can understand that. That's why when I heard the news down at the station, my main concern was you." Trouble couldn't help but to respect her for being down. She could have easily got him flipped. Trouble knew right then that Tameka would do anything to keep him by her side. Trouble looked Tameka in her eyes and said "So you're crazy in love with me." "Yes, I am," she replied "And you will do anything I tell you to," he said lifting up her chin so he can get a good look in her eyes.

"Like a rushing bullet," She replied wrapping her arms around Troubles neck. "Take off them clothes," he said giving her an order. Tameka did what she was told, standing there in a lace black thong set. Trouble then turned her around with her back facing him.

"You know the boss hates to fight with underwear," he whispered in her ear. Tameka quickly came out her panties and unfastened her bra, tossing everything on the couch. Standing there with nothing on, Troubles dick was rock hard. "Now get on that couch in position," Trouble said pulling off his shirt. Tameka walked over then got on top of the couch, arching her back with her ass poked out. Trouble pulled out his dick and then told Tameka to spread her ass cheeks apart. She did exactly what she was told and spread her ass cheeks apart, as far as she could, exposing her pink hole. Trouble ran his tongue across his top lip aiming his stiff dick at her wet hole before diving in. He then bit down on her neck before giving her one big smack on her ass cheeks.

"Ahhhh... Baby," she moaned as he continued to handle that kitty the way only he could.

CHAPTER 11: EL MAYO'S DAUGHTER

As Nitro pulled up in front of El Mayo's mansion, he got out and stepped up to the door, grabbing a huge metal ring and banged it a few times. The door came open- 6-foot, one inch tall and approximately 145 pounds, all curves- Mylene smiled when she saw Nitro standing right before her eyes. Mylene was Filipino and Mexican. She wore her hair long, black and curly. Her features were exotic; beautiful long legs, small waist, fat ass and double D breasts, leading up to a round face with chinky eyes, a thin nose and pretty glossed lips.

"Hello," Mylene said as she opened the door wider allowing Nitro to enter the mansion. Nitro was coming by more often sitting down with El Mayo's daughter and talking business. Mylene had owned a couple of motels on south beach strip. Mylene reminded Nitro of Brenda. She was smart when it came to finances, investing, and her money. Nitro knew that Mylene was on his trail because every time he stopped by, she would make heavy eye contact with him. Nitro didn't want to disrespect El Mayo by messing with his daughter, but his thing was, if she comes his way like she wanted to taste the magic stick, then he was going to put it in her life.

"I got a call from your father telling me to come by," Nitro said as his eyes roamed down to her crotch area. Mylene was standing there in a pair orange terry cloth booty shorts and a matching tank top. The frigid air displayed her erect nipples which stood up in his face like a welcome committee.

"Please come," Mylene said as she extended her hand. Nitro took her hand in his, he stepped inside letting the door close behind him. Both walked up a brown and tan marble staircase that led to the top balcony where you can get a good view of the Atlantic Ocean.

"God damn!" Nitro mumbled as he watched her ass shift and jiggle as she walked up the stairs. Nitro knew something was up because he never went this far through the house. Both made it up on the top balcony. Nitro seen a large glass sliding door that led to a master bedroom. Nitro thought to himself this shit is nice when he looked down and noticed a large stretch pool. Four large golden lion heads were on each corner of the pool. Across from it was a large glass table with a throne-like chair on each end with a gold chess set in the middle.

Mylene turned to face Nitro and said, "I want you to fuck me really good over the balcony," as she put her tongue down Nitro's throat. Nitro's dick got straight hard when he heard those words come out of Mylene's mouth.

"I can't Mylene," Nitro said.

"Why not? Because of my father? Are you scared of my father?" she replied stepping closer to him. "Don't worry about my father, I am a big girl. Now bend me over on this balcony and get this pussy," she said before sucking on Nitro's ear lobe. Mylene stripped down all her clothes until she was completely naked. She then walked over to the balcony, bending over, exposing her clean shaved cherry. Nitro felt like Mylene had disrespected him by telling him that he feared her father. He knew deep down in is heart that he wasn't scared of anyone that walked the planet earth. Nitro stripped down out his clothes and walked over with his dick standing at attention. Nitro spread Mylene's fat ass cheeks apart and entered her fully from behind. Mylene closed her eyes and bit down on her bottom lip.

"Ummm," she moaned.

"That's right, take this dick," he whispered in her ear.

The feeling of Mylene's warmth wrapped around his dick like a blanket. He started feeling so damn good that he found himself in sync with her, stroking her softly. In and out, the strokes became faster and more passionate until Nitro found himself hammering away at Mylene's pussy like a jackrabbit on steroids. Mylene had gripped the balcony real tight as Nitro pounded away on her pussy. Her screams were heard, catching one of the security guard's attention, making him look up at the balcony. He was surprised at what he was witnessing. The security guard reached inside his pocket quickly pulling out his I-Phone, aiming it towards Nitro and Mylene. He then pushed his video button to record the whole play. Nitro continued to pound Mylene from the back making her moans get louder and cocking her ass up, taking in all that Nitro had to offer. In the heat of the moment she called out in between moans, "Nitro, oooh baby." He gripped her tightly around her waist and whispered in her ear. "What's my name?" he asked, pumping her hard, as if he was stabbing her with his dick, waiting for a response in between thrusts.

"Nitro," she barely got the words out as the pains of passion ran through every bone in her body.

"Whose pussy is this now?" he asked her surprisingly. "It's … Nitro, Nitro," she moaned. "It's …It's you baby?" "whose?" he asked as he punished her forcefully. Throughout her whole 25 years she had never had it laid down to her like Nitro was laying it down.

"Its…it's Nit… Nitro's." she said. "It's yours, baby." "For how long?" he asked, enjoying every minute of Mylene's sweet pussy.

"Huh" she asked, caught up in the sexcapade.

"I said, for how long?" he began hitting a spot that she never knew existed. "How long is this pussy mine?"

"Forever and ever, until death do us part."

"Don't say that unless its official."

"Nitro, it is, and that's on everything. I love you. Nitro, this is your pussy." She said as she stepped up her game, poppin that pussy like she was one of Luke's dancers. All Mylene's girlfriends were black, so she learned how to please a man at a young age. She told herself that she could have easily been a porn star. Her fuck game was on point.

"Beat this pussy baby, this is your pussy now." She said.

"oooohhh, you better mean it," he said, thrusting in and out of her. Hearing the name Nitro only made his dick harder. Nitro nut was boiling inside of him like a volcano about to erupt.

"Thats right, this is Nitro's pussy. This is my pussy. Oh shit," he moaned as he felt his cream running through his veins. He pulled out and let it shoot all over Mylene's ass like it was a tsunami. As the white thick cum oozed out of his big black stallion, Mylene quickly fell to her knees, taking the sexual session to the highest level, completely throwing Nitro off balance when she licked every ounce of the cum she could manage to lick off his dick and swallowed it like it was Kool-Aid. When it was all said and done, Nitro said "Wow!" Mylene was a straight up and down freak, who he thought was such an innocent girl.

CHAPTER 12:
SNITCHES GET STITCHES...OR BULLETS

IT WAS A WEDNESDAY AFTERNOON PACMAN AND HIS baby mother were downtown St. Pete, walking their four-year-old son. When an all-black tinted Cadillac s4 pulled up behind them. Sebastian jumped out the car with a Russian AK-47 Rifle with a Banana Clip, letting off several rounds "Chop! Chop! Cha! Chop! Cha! Cha!" sounds of gunshots roared, echoing through the sky as Sebastian dumped the whole clip into the family. Never letting his eyes leave his target. Pacman and his baby mother with their son, was stretched out on the sidewalk. Sebastian saw the life leaving Pacman's eyes as he lay on the ground beside his son. With a wicked smile he said, "Game over snitch," Then he quickly jumped back inside the car leaving the scene.

Nitro was getting ready to walk out the door when breaking news broadcast across his television, making him come to a stand-still.

"Hi, this is Grace Wright reporting live from Bay Walk, in downtown St. Petersburg, where a deadly shooting just took place.

Two adults and a four-year-old child has been shot and killed. No one knows the motive behind the shooting but right now officers are still investigating trying to put pieces together and find out who could have done something like this. Again, two adults and a four-year-old boy has been gunned down in broad day light." Nitro shook his head, before walking out the door. He didn't have any feeling on what just happened to Pacman's baby mother and child. That's one thing Nitro didn't like, a snitch. He didn't have a problem giving Trouble the order to kill Pacman. He let Trouble know wherever he at, that's where he will lay. Now he is just waiting on Angie to call and give him more information on who was behind the set up.

Angie walked into Captain Andrew's office. Carrying a black suitcase, wearing a tight fitted black Chanel dress with off black stockings and black pumps. Angie took a seat down in front of Captain Andrew's desk with her legs crossed and game face on. Captain Andrew was just getting off the phone, when he recognized Angie walked into his office.

"Ms. Brown, how can I help you today?" "Yes, you can first tell me why are my people being watched? I thought we had a deal," Angie said with a concerned look.

"Where did you hear that information from?" Captain Andrew replied.

"I have my inside connect." She replied with a smirk. Captain Andrew quickly picked up his office phone and called Detective Green, to find out what was going on.

"Why haven't you got back with me? Like I ordered you to. I told you don't do anything until you get with me first," Captain Andrew bawled out then slammed down the phone.

"Ms. Brown, I am sorry for what took place I wasn't aware of what went down, it will not happen again," he said as he looked Angie in her eyes, hoping she forgives him. He didn't want to break the contract that he agreed to. Angie was supplying him with the best product money could buy. Every time Angie got a shipment in, she fixed up a self-package for Captain Andrew to get his high on. The drugs were so potent, Captain Andrew would get high at least three times a day.

The contract was, if he kept law enforcements off GMC, Angie would keep him straight.

"I am pretty sure, that we will not have this problem again," She said before raising out of her seat and straightening her dress. Captain Andrew nodded his head as he watched Angie put the black suitcase on top of his desk. She then opened the suitcase. What Captain Andrew had in front of his face was ten circles of cooked up crack cocaine, with twenty small glass pipes lined up, side by side. Captain Andrew's mouth got watery when he saw the drugs. Captain Andrew was about to reach for a circle when he was stopped by Angie slamming down the top of the suitcase.

"Wait just a minute cowboy, before I give you anything out this suitcase. I need information on the two detectives that are watching GMC and where they stay."

Captain Andrew leaned back into his chair and thought hard about what Angie just asked of him. He knew if he gave her the information that she needed he would never see them two detectives again. Captain Andrew's addiction was so heavy on his back at the time, he didn't care if he gave Angie the detectives addresses. What he did know was that she wasn't leaving his office with that suitcase. Captain Andrew turned his computer towards him and typed in a four-digit number. All the information for the officers and detectives popped up on his screen he then scrolled down until he found what he was looking for "Damn it!," he said to himself as he clicked on the wrong name. Captain Andrew hit the back button taking him back to the top of the page. "Fuck, just give me a minute I will have that for you in a second," he said as he scrolled back down and clicked on the two names, then clicked the mouse button to print.

Angie waited with her left hand on her hip for Captain Andrew to give her what she asked for.

"Okay, that will do it," he said getting up from his desk walking over to the printer. Captain Andrew handed Angie a slip with the detective's information. She folded it and placed it in her bra.

"Thank you," she said before walking out of his office with a grin on her face. Captain Andrew opened the suitcase with his goodies inside, ready to beam up to Scotti.

CHAPTER 13: MYLENE

"**B**RA, THE PUSSY WAS GOOD, I JUST HOPE SHE DON'T GO letting her father know what took place because she came on to me," Nitro said as he rolled up a blunt.

"Man fuck that, what can he do? She gave the pussy up. It's not like you put a gun to her head and took the pussy." Nitro nodded his head agreeing to what trouble was saying.

"You right bra, I just don't want that to fuck up our business we got going on," Nitro said before licking the end of the blunt. Trouble passed him the fire and said "Fuck that wet back, he haven't went down on the price yet and we been copping fifty to sixty bricks at a time." Nitro's phone began vibrating inside of his pocket before he pulled it out to see who was calling. He recognized that he just got a text from Angie who had Detective White & Detective Green's info. Nitro then smiled to himself before letting Trouble know what just came through.

"Okay, we're going to send the Pirate Kids at them dick suckers," Trouble said taking hits off the blunt, before handing it to Nitro.

"So, Lil' Mama told you straight up that you have to kill Pacman huh?"

"Yeah," Trouble replied.

"That's, what's up. I bet you were pissing in your pants when she told you that she was a cop," Nitro said laughing.

"Hell yeah I was, I almost whacked her ass," Trouble replied with a serious look.

"Bra, she makes a good weapon for the team, don't fuck that shit up."

"I won't bra, that baby is fucked up about me. She said that she will do anything I tell her to," Trouble said reaching in his pocket pulling out his phone, checking to see if he had any missed calls. "Word, she can give us the inside on a lot of shit now," Nitro stated.

CHAPTER 14: FALLEN "HEROES"

IT WAS A THURSDAY AFTERNOON, 3PM WHEN DETECTIVE Green and his wife stepped out, getting ready to head to the beach. Both got inside the car when an all-white Hyundai pulled up on the driver side of Detective Green, letting down the dark tinted window, exposing a brown skinned girls face.

"Yes, can I help you?" Detective Green asked.

"Yes Sir, I am from out of town and I am lost, can you please give me directions on how to get to Gulfport."

"Yes, I can help you with that," Detective Green said sticking his head out the window, pointing his finger, letting the girl know what avenue to jump on. The back side of the Hyundai window rolled down, before Detective Green could get his last word out, the double barrel shot gun let out one big blast, sending Detective Green's brains into his wife's lap. All she could do was scream but was quickly silenced by a slug to her face before the all-white Hyundai took off.

Later that day, Detective White stepped out of his car and into his house, closing the door behind him when he felt a heavy object hit his head and then he saw black.

"Wake up Pig." Detective White heard the loud commanding voice say, struggling to open his eyes and lift his head. He sat half-way up and got the shock of his life. Sebastian stood over him with a gun in his hand.

"What the fuck!" he mumbled. He tried to move his hand, but it was cuffed behind his back. Detective White yanked his shackled hands, trying to break free.

"What are you doing kid?" he asked, trying to sit up straight and as he did so, blood started pouring down his forehead. Detective White tried to speak as calm as possible. "Okay kid, tell me what you want from me?"

"Your soul," Sebastian replied as he held his gun up and then squeezed down on the trigger letting four hollow points enter his chest. Sebastian then picked up the brown bag that had five bricks inside. The same drugs Detective White seized from Pacman at the traffic stop. Sebastian took one more look at Detective White's lifeless body, making sure he didn't see any type of movement. He knows officers can fake like they were dead, that's what they were trained to do. Not with Sebastian, he let off one more shot, making sure he was dead before fleeing the scene.

CHAPTER 15: MIKO

(10:30PM)

TROUBLE WAS RIDING DOWN THIRTY FOURTH STREET north with snow beside him. Trouble recognized Miko's sky Blue Lexus 350 sitting in Red Lobsters parking lot.

"I got this pussy," Trouble said to himself as he busted a u-turn, pulling up inside the parking lot, parking his car across from Miko's. Trouble spotted Miko and his girl walking through the parking lot towards his car.

"Bae, listen to me. I got to have this pussy ass nigga, so sit tight," Trouble said pulling out his Glock 40, cocking the hammer back, putting one inside the chamber. Snow nodded her head and continued to roll a blunt. She already knew anytime Trouble had a problem, no matter where they were at, Trouble was going to take care of that problem, no matter who he is with. Trouble had exited the vehicle, ducking down real low, creeping with his fire out in his hand, ready to squeeze. Miko looked to his right and saw Trouble creeping towards him, that's when he reached for his gun from his waist line.

Trouble let off the first three shot's, "Boc! Boc! Boc!" missing his target. Miko took the girl he was with and used her for a shield. Miko bust five shots back Pow! Pow! Pow! Pow! Pow! Making Trouble crouch behind a car. The girl that was with Miko was stretched out on the ground with a bullet wound to her chest and throat. Miko ran and got behind a car as well dropping his keys. The whole parking lot was like the wild wild west, bullets flying everywhere. Boc! Boc! Boc! Boc! … Pow! Pow! Pow! Pow!

Trouble and Miko were having a real live shoot out inside the parking lot, making people get down on the floor inside the restaurant.

Miko let off four more shots before his brain got blown out his head. Snow released one single shot, sending a slug ripping through the right side of Miko's head, spatting the car door with blood and tissue.

"Pussy Ass Bitch," Snow said with her smoking gun in hand. Trouble looked up and viewed Snow standing over Miko's body. He then ran over with a grin on his face.

"That's what I am talking about Baby, you cook that Mutha Fucker," Trouble said giving Snow a compliment for ending the gun fight. That was Snow's first body and she wouldn't mind doing it again. Both got back inside the car and took off from the scene.

Nitro got a call from Trouble letting him know that Miko is no longer in service. Nitro had managed to do what no other hustler in St. Pete had ever achieved, taking over the North and South sides. He offered the best dope at the cheapest price and like any successful businessman, he created a brand, labeling his coke

"Madonna." Everyone craved for it. He was getting it cheap, he didn't have to mark it up too high. El Mayo finally came down on the coke price from ten a key to eight thousand a block. Even the heroin price dropped as well, from seventeen to ten. The empire had spread throughout Florida and a lot of different cities. Nitro had quickly turned the $800,000 that he had left over from two years of losses and turned it into $4 million in a small amount of time. His relationship with Mylene was strong and he had the Streets on lock. El Mayo still didn't know that Nitro was plugging his daughter.

Nitro had recently purchased courtside season tickets to the Miami Heat Game, where he and Mylene loved to spend their nights as a couple. During the days, Mylene was your typical kept woman. She wanted for nothing, drove high-end cars and did a lot of shopping for clothes by designers with names that are hard to pronounce, but in addition to being a diva, she was also very domesticated. She made sure she stayed on top of the numerous contractors that she'd hired to do renovations to their new home and she also found the time to cook daily. Nitro felt on top of the world at this point. He even managed to recruit some of Miko's old workers and place them under his organization. Everyone wanted to get a piece of the American dream and with Nitro's prices and high-quality product, they were more than able to. What Nitro didn't know was a new hustler, by the name Gunz was in town. Gunz was from New York City but had a coke plug in Jersey. He heard about St. Pete through a friend telling him how the money was so sweet down there. Gunz and his hit squad crew rounded up and took a trip down. Gunz didn't know that Nitro and his GMC clique had already put the city on lock. Sooner or later Gunz will meet his match.

CHAPTER 16: THE TRUTH IS REVEALED

NITRO WAS SITTING INSIDE HIS CONDO ON TREASURE Island, having a conversation with Angie, trying to figure out why he hasn't received any shipment yet. Angie was already aware of Nitro sleeping with Mylene. She didn't like the fact that Mylene pushed herself onto him. She thought that her and Nitro had something going on beside business. So, Angie got into her feelings and stopped Nitro from receiving any work from El Mayo.

"Angie what's going on? Why haven't we received any work yet?" Nitro said with a deadpan look.

"Look Nitro, I already know that you and Mylene got something going on, so I stopped everything until you give me some answers," she replied with a serious look on her face.

"What the fuck you mean, you stopped everything," Nitro said loudly.

"Hold up Baby, lower your voice when you're talking to me," Angie ordered.

"Look Angie, I am missing a lot of money and you sitting here telling me you stopped everything because you think me and Mylene got something going on."

"No, I don't think shit, I have proof," she said reaching inside her handbag and pulling out her cell phone, pushing the play button.

"How can you explain this." Nitro was lost for words when he saw the video of him and Mylene having sex.

"So now you trying to black male me," Nitro said with his face balled up, sitting straight up in his seat.

"No Nitro, I am not trying to blackmail you, I thought what we had was strong," she replied with a puppy face.

"Listen Angie, what we got going on is business, nothing personal. Okay we did our thing and that's cool, but I still have to keep it business," Nitro said, letting Angie know that he is about his money.

"Nitro, I killed my best friend for you and on top of that, don't forget I made you to be who you are today. So, come back to earth," She said in an aggressive tone.

"I understand that Angie—" "No, you don't understand," Angie said standing up before cutting Nitro off from finishing his sentence. She then walked towards him and climbed on top of him.

"Okay, this the play. You are going to give me this dick and then you going to cut the bitch loose, or I will do it for you. I am pretty sure El Mayo wouldn't like it if the same person he is selling weight to, be putting dick down his daughter's throat," Angie said, sticking her tongue inside of Nitro's ear. Nitro wanted to stop what was taking place, but the pleasure was so heavy in the air, so he just gave in. Angie fumbled with Nitro's belt buckle, before letting the bulldog out his cage. She stroked his dick to get him ready for what was about to go down. Nitro lifted her Dolce & Gabbana dress up over her head and then tossed it to the side, exposing her smooth chocolate skin. "I want you to fuck me right," she whispered in Nitro's ear. She took his nine-inch pole and slid it off inside her wet box. She rode him slow, going up and down.

"Mmmm ... Ssss ..." She moaned as she clenched her eyes shut, trying to adjust to his size. As every curve of her pussy caressed his dick and he looked up into her face and seen that she was enjoying the pleasure he was giving her. He relished every stroke. He wanted to keep slow stroking her, but her body was asking for more, so he had to answer the call.

"Nitro," she repeated as he picked up speed, slamming her ass down, triggering her orgasm to come on fast. Then within seconds he had found that spot and knew just how to work it. Angie held his shoulders tight as her whole body became overwhelmed with pleasure

"Yes, give it to me," She moaned loudly as she began to cum all over his dick.

"I want you to spread my legs wide," she looked down and said to him as Nitro still pumped off inside her. He pulled out of Angie with her thick white cum all over his dick, looking like a snow cone. She stood up and got in position. Nitro grabbed both of her legs and spread them apart as far as they can go. Nitro stroked his dick making it harder. Angie watched as each vein bulged. The look in his eyes let her know he was planning to put her out of her misery.

"Damn, that feels good," she moaned as he slipped his middle finger inside her. When he felt her muscles constrict, he pulled out his finger and slipped her a few inches of that dick. Angie tensed up as he began going deeper.

"Oh shit! Nitro, wait!" She pleaded as he began breaking down the wall. Angie was on the brink, she tried to ease up from Nitro, but he locked his grip, refusing to allow her to slow down his rhythm.

"Nitro, you are pounding me to hard," she reached her hand on his stomach to slow his push. Nitro pushed her hand away and continued to pound her

"Nitro, wait" she moaned.

"Oh no, you told me to fuck you right, so that's what it is," he replied showing no mercy. He was hitting Angie spot with straight pressure

"Yes … Just like that," she moaned.

"You want it like this?"

"Yes, like that," Nitro positioned her legs, putting them both on top of his shoulders. He then dug back inside her.

"Oh … shit, baby." She moaned.

"That's right, beat this pussy," she said as she dug her nails into Nitro's back. He looked down at her body glistening with his sweat.

"Get that ass up and let me pound that cake from the back again." He pulled out of her slippery wet hole and stroked his dick, keeping it hard. Angie stood up as ordered and got in position, bending over grabbing a hold of the two couch arms. Nitro got behind and slammed his dick back into her sloppy, wet, juicy, pussy "Ahhhhh … yesssssss … fuck me, fuck me hard," she cried out. Angie's pussy juice ran down her legs like a water fall as he took five more pumps, before releasing his load all over her back.

CHAPTER 17: GUNZ

Gunz pulled into the garage of his side chick's penthouse and parked next to a Midnight Blue, BMW 650 Coup. He exited his Bentley Continental GT and flipped through his keys to open the garage door. Walking through the large living room, Gunz began loosening his tie. He went to a bedroom and peeped out the window.

"She a bad motherfucker," He spoke under his breath. Baby Phat was sporting a pair of Gucci shades, lying on a beach chair. She was reading a king magazine with a picture of her gracing the cover. The young video vixen had the face of Meagan Good and the body of Beyonce but she stayed in more drama than Wendy Williams. Gunz had met her at a strip club that she used to work at, before shaking her body in hip hop videos. He began undressing, carefully laying his clothes on her bed. He grabbed a pair of his Calvin Klein trunks from the closet, slipped them on and headed outside. His bare feet trailed the wet tiles on the sun baked patio. He leaned down and painted a kiss on Baby Phat's lips, then laid on the lounge chair beside her.

"How many times you gonna look at that magazine?" he asked.

"However many times it takes for me to understand why these rapper's wives are beefing on my blog. Every fucking day, all about my interview."

"You know how them hatin ass bitches be," Gunz said, palming one of her large silicone-filled breasts. He laughed.

"Stop," she swatted his hand.

"Broads just hatin! that's what the fuck it is!"

"That's the logical outcome of admitting in the pages of a National Magazine that you had a married rappers face between your legs."

"A Million Motherfuckers is calling themself MC-this and MC-that. I fuck one mother fuckin rapper and I'm a ho. Broads all scared of me and shit."

"Them pictures of you posing damn near naked in front of this house he paid for on that Mercedes old boy gave you, can easily make freaks nervous."

"Fuck'em all." Baby Phat dropped the magazine and her shades on a small table and stood up. She walked to the edge of the pool, her butt cheeks jiggling with each step. She slowly eased out of her bathing suit, then turned to Gunz

"Come and get me." She dove into the water.

"This freak got me chasing the pussy, literally," he mumbled.

"Watch when I catch her ass." He quickly peeled out of his trunks as he stood up. His dick rose while he was staring at Baby Phat's breasts. She was leaning in the corner furthest from him in the pool. Even with 15 yards separating them, he could see the sun glistening off her wet body.

Gunz dove into the pool and swam toward her. As he closed in on her, she took off. He swam after her. She circled past him with a smile. Gunz pursued her, but she went under water and slipped past him again, popping up in another corner. "This fucking freak got me going in circles."

"Guess I'll just let you get it." She said. Climbing up on the edge of the pool. She spread her legs wide, her feet dangling beneath the cold water. Gunz focused on her thick thighs. He saw the thin layer of hair covering her pussy glowing with droplets of water as he got closer to her. She laid back. Gunz stood on the steps that lined the entire wall at the bottom of the pool. He grabbed her thighs and planted his face between them. Baby Phat let out a moan and her body jerked. Gunz slithered his tongue around her clit, then inside of her. Her legs wrapped around his neck as his tongue overpowered her. Her body began to quake. Next came the flow of her juices into his mouth, then her legs fell from his neck back into the water. Gunz looked up, gazing at her flawless frame. He was laughing inside. He always found it comical how easy it was for him to subdue Baby Phat's 32-22-38 physique with a few swipes of his tongue. He had never met a woman he could make cum so quickly.

"You the motha fucking man, Gunz," she whispered as she leaned up on her elbows. She inched forward and wrapped her arms around Gunz's neck, while slipping into the pool. Gunz eased inside of her. He grabbed both butt cheeks as her legs wrapped around his waist. Then he suddenly pinned her to the wall and began pumping. Water splashed violently with each of his strokes. He winced when her long fingernails dug into his back.

"You the motha fuckin man," she yelled. Gunz rammed harder. He was about to cum.

Her legs clenched him tighter as he released a load. She squeezed her legs tighter around him as his body went limp.

"Damn," she moaned. "Your shit is strong. I can feel your nut up in me."

"Oh shit," Gunz thought. As they parted, he grabbed his dick. "What the fuck!" Until then, he had not had sex without a condom in over a year. The last time he did he had to coax an old flame into having an abortion. Child support cases are the only things Gunz hated more than cops and snitches.

"You hungry?" Baby Phat asked.

"I'm about to make me something to eat. You sucked all the damn energy out me, so I need to re-up."

"I gotta go."

"Mother fucker, you just got here!" Gunz's mind was so focused on a possible pregnancy that Baby Phat's tone of voice didn't upset him. He climbed out of the pool and walked off.

"So, you just bust a nut and break out? I aint one of them hood rats you be fucking with, Gunz!"

"I gotta take care of something," Gunz responded. He had been seeing Baby Phat for almost a year. Her home was his second residence and her cooking was something he craved each time he was there. He spent the night in her Villa at least twice a week. He had his own key. A closet full of clothes, plus a towel, rag and toothbrush in her bathroom. He had practically moved in. But it was the first time he was leaving after staying less than a few hours. Gunz sped up his pace entering the Villa. He made his way to the bedroom, where he had undressed and put on some fresh clothes. He had just finished lacing his brown Salvatore Ferragamo shoes, when Baby Phat burst through the door like a stick-up kid in a drug spot.

"This is some real bullshit." She pointed at him. She flailed her arms aimlessly as she barked about Gunz treating her like a hoe. Her eyes were bulging, and her head was bouncing like a bobble head doll. She was naked, still dripping water from the pool.

Gunz jumped up. "Look, baby. I ain't walking out your life, I'm just walking out the door. Good thing about it is, you can go out and in, so I'll be back."

"Nah, fuck that!" she jumped in front of the door and folded her arms. She twisted her head back and forth.

"You ain't walkin' out this mother fuckin' door." Gunz stepped toward her. He put his hand on her shoulder.

"Why you playing, girl? Games are for kids and athletes and neither one of us play with toys or balls. So, let's stop the bull shit." Baby Phat gritted her teeth and slapped Gunz arms, knocking his hand off her. Before his hand fell to his side, his other hand had instinctively slapped her. Baby Phat flew into a nearby dresser. She scrambled to her feet, knocking her jewelry box and bottles of perfume off the dresser to the carpeted floor. "Oh shit. What the fuck did I just do?" Gunz heart sunk into his chest. He wanted to apologize, but that would do little to change what he had unintentionally done.

Tears trickled down Baby Phat's face. She stood up, silently. Her mouth was open, her upper lip bleeding, she looked like a frightened animal. She slowly backed into a corner away from Gunz. She was curled into the fetal position. Gunz walked out of her room and her house. As he drove home, he regretted that he lost control. He was a womanizer, but not a woman beater. He had trained himself to control woman with a slick tongue and stiff dick. His violent outburst was a sign that he had lost all control. Just like him chasing after Baby Phat and having sex with her without a condom. He knew that he had made a big mistake by going in her raw.

CHAPTER 18: BLACKMAILED

IT WAS A SUNDAY NIGHT, AND NITRO WAS SITTING ON THE couch watching television, smoking a blunt. Trying to get Angie out of his head. Him and Mylene had just got in a small argument, so he didn't want to be fucked with. Nitro been meeting up with Angie more often, laying down the pipe, just to keep her mouth shut. Now, she started to get on his nerves with all the calling and coming by his house without notice. Nitro was on the verge of saying fuck it, but he knew if he did, his business with El Mayo would be dead and probably start a war. Nitro felt like Angie was getting out of hand. He could not believe that he had sex with her while Mylene was in the other bedroom sleep. He knew if he didn't do something about the situation, things would get ugly. Nitro knew he was wrong for messing around with Angie and taking their business to the next level by meeting up with her to fulfill her sexual needs. He figured by feeding Angie the dick that she would keep her mouth closed.

Mylene was in the kitchen cooking some fried shrimps and potatoes. Nitro stood in the doorway watching Mylene's ass cheeks jiggle at the bottom of his T-shirt, as she stirred the vegetables in the pan. Instantly his dick rocked up. Feeling his presence, she turned and looked over her shoulder.

"Hey, babe, you just can't wait. You smell this good cooking coming through the living room, don't you?" she said with a grin.

"I sure do," he replied coming up behind her.

"I am almost done, give me a minute." Mylene went back to stirring the food.

"I got what, I want to eat right here in front of me," he said as he began to run his hands up her legs.

"Nitro, stop. you're going to get something started." He nibbled on her neck as he pressed against her. Mylene arched her back. She could feel him rising against her. Closing her eyes, she enjoyed the warmth of his lips on the nape of her neck.

"Pay attention. You might burn yourself." He said as he moved his hands to her breasts.

"Be good. I thought you wanted to eat." She slid his hand back down.

"I want some back talk first," he released his dick from his gym shorts and spread her legs with his foot.

"Nitro, you're gonna make me burn the food." He placed his hand on her side and began nibbling on her shoulder.

"Fuck that food," he whispered in her ear, beginning to pull her away from the stove. Mylene quickly turned forward. Gripping the counter, she braced herself to feel every inch of his power. Easing in between her sweet walls, he released a breath and a small moan.

"Damn Baby, this pussy feels good."

"I know," She moaned, as he began to stroke her just right. Within minutes, he found and pleasured her spot. Mylene lowered her head as he gripped her hips and devoured her as if he hadn't had her in months. Nitro was in a zone. Her every moan only made him stroke harder and faster. Mylene's grasp tightened with every forceful movement. "Niiit… be gentle," she pleaded, He was on the edge, ignoring her call for mercy. He continued to slide in her wetness, not missing a wall on the way in or out.

"Shit!" He said as he began to bust long and hard. As the last drop drained from his body, he pushed all the way in.

Mylene inhaled as he ran his soft tongue along her neck and back.

"Damn, Ma. that pussy is soakin wet. I'ma need more of that," he whispered in her ear as he pulled out. Taking his dick in his hand, he began stroking himself back to full potential.

"Baby, wait!" she turned toward him. Again, ignoring her, Nitro kissed her hungrily.

"Baby," she called out, but Nitro was focused as if she hadn't said a word. Grabbing her waist, he placed her up on the counter and stood between her legs. Fitting perfectly between her thighs.

"Nitro," she moaned as he began to tear at her T-shirt, releasing her breasts. Placing his mouth over her nipple, he sucked gently as he slid in fast and hard. Mylene grabbed at his shirt as he hit the bottom with every forceful blow. Moving back, Mylene tried to escape all those inches. "Come here," he growled, Pulling her back to the edge of the counter. Sensing her struggle, he grabbed her legs and threw them over his shoulders. Holding her in place, he went to work, again finding it hard to hold back.

The pussy was wetter than a sponge. After about twenty more minutes, he was again on edge.

"Ssss … baby, baby, baby, baby," he moaned as he again released his passion all the way inside her. Mylene arched her back and received all of him. Out of breath and satisfied, Nitro pulled her to him kissing and sucking her lips, he looked in her eyes.

"Let's go finish this session off in the bat cave," he said removing the front part of Mylene's hair from her eyes.

"What are you waiting for?" she replied with a grin. She grabbed him around his neck and wrapped her leg's around his waist and held on tight as he carried her away.

CHAPTER 19: FLAKA

GUNZ HAD DROVE DOWN TO BELLE GLADE, FLORIDA to meet his connect. Hector called and asked him to meet at the spot and Gunz was really hoping it was for a good reason. Hector was a short, brown skinned, muscular type, with blonde, slicked back hair. He came straight from Columbia, off the banana boat. Hector was 17 when he came to American but started to hustle at the age of 19. Gunz first met Hector at the urban source awards, then they both exchanged numbers and stayed in contact ever since.

Big cookie opened the large steel door to the warehouse. Letting Hector pull in his new 2014 Jaguar CT. A light-brown skinned girl stepped out of the passenger's side, wearing some sky blue cut off jean shorts, with an ass so fat, the jeans she was wearing were about to burst open. She then walked to the driver's side and opened the door. Hector stepped out the car wearing a black silk, Gucci, button up dress shirt. A pair of loose slacks, with some all black gators on. Gunz had on his game face waiting to see what the lick will be. After getting a good view of the female, Gunz can see that she was a Latino chick. Hector always kept him some badass Latino girls around. He never stepped out his race. Hector felt like Latino girls had the sweetest pussy. After opening the door for Hector, the girl walked towards the back of the car and opened the trunk. Gunz noticed the gun she had tucked behind her back.

"Hey, my friend, happy that you made it down," Hector said in his native accent, with a Cuban cigar hanging out of his mouth.

"I hope this shit is worth my time, I was about to drive in some pussy," Gunz said rubbing his hands together.

"Don't worry my friend, you will have all the pussy in the world, once this hit the Streets," Hector replied with a smile. Hector grabbed the black handbag out the truck and unzipped it, grabbing one block out. He then grabbed a straight edge razor from his top shirt pocket and sliced through the thick gray duct tape.

"This right here my friend is call FLAKA, the next highest level of drugs. Eighty five percent of Detroit's population is on this drug. This new drug right here is bringing in major bucks."

Gunz looked at the rocked-up crystal brick and said "So you telling me right now, this drug is nowhere in the state of Florida?" Gunz asked with a serious look.

"Yes, that is exactly what I am trying to tell you. You will be the first with this product." he replied back. All Gunz can see is dollar signs. He knew once he hit St. Pete with this powerful drug, the shop will be shut down for other local hustlers in the game.

"So, what's the ticket?" Gunz asked.

"I have ten blocks. I want fifteen thousand apiece. So that will be one hundred and fifty thousand," Hector replied.

"Okay, that's not a problem. NYC!" Gunz called out. NYC breezed in from around the corner carrying a brown leather Louis Vuitton bag. Wearing an all-black, body cat suit, designed by Ms.Cat. NYC is eye candy, with a high yellow skin complexion, light brown eyes, measurements 34-26-42 and height 5'7. She always rocked her hair in a different color Mohawk. NYC handed the bag over to the Latino girl, giving her a lustful look. Making her smile. NYC had her share of both worlds. She kept her a set of beautiful girls around and wouldn't have a problem adding Hector's girl to her list.

"There's three hundred thousand in the bag. So, when you touch the other ten blocks, make sure they find their way to me," Gunz said with a serious look.

"No problem," he replied. Gunz never had a problem giving Hector his money firsthand.

Gunz been doing business with Hector for a while now and ever since then things been straight.

CHAPTER 20: NO MORE HIDING

"**D**AMN BABY, WHAT AM I GOING TO DO WITH YOU?"
Mylene said breathless.

"Love me, that's all you can do. What the fuck you be doing to your pussy?" Nitro asked almost out of breath as well. Like he been running from the cops.

"Nothing baby, I just got that come back, sweet potato pie pussy," she replied giggling.

"You definitely got that, just make sure you hide me from your father because I don't want you to find me floating somewhere in a lake."

"Oh my God, you are crazy. Ain't nobody going to find you floating in no lake. Besides, I want to let my father know about our relationship," She said with a smile.

"No Mylene, listen. I respect your father a lot, but I don't think you need to tell him," Nitro said with a serious look.

"Why baby? I am happy with you and on top of that I done fell in love with you. So, if he can't accept that and know that you are the one for me, then he can't accept me," she said with a deadpan look. Nitro thought for a split second on what Mylene was talking about. She really fell in love with him in a short period of time.

"Baby he needs to know about us and I am tired of hiding our relationship. Now stop worrying about my father and come over here and get some more of this sweet potato pie," She said in her sexist tone of voice. Mylene had put a grin on Nitro's face. As soon as he was about to get between Mylene's legs, his phone rang. Mylene had sucked her teeth when she heard Nitro's phone go off. Nitro grabbed his phone off the nightstand and answered it without looking at his caller ID.

"Hello."

"I need to see you right away. I have a water leak that needs to be plugged," Angie said as she rotated two fingers on her clit making herself come to another climax. Angie let out a little moan over the phone, letting Nitro know what she was doing at the time.

"Right now? I can't," he said watching Mylene break up some weed into a split cigar.

"Boy what you mean, that you can't right now. You better get over here and on top of that, we need to talk on some business," She said grabbing a damp wash cloth, cleaning around her pussy.

"Okay, I will be there in 20 minutes."

"Make it fifteen," she replied and then hung up.

Nitro heard the clink sound go off in his ear.

"Baby, I will be back, I got some business to take care of." Nitro got out of bed putting his clothes on.

"But Baby, I thought it was our night." She said with the puppy face.

"Don't worry baby, I will make it up to you." He replied throwing his Burberry shirt over his head.

"So, what you want me to do with this," she said holding up the rolled blunt.

"Get high, I will be right back." He replied before giving Mylene a kiss and grabbing his keys off the nightstand and walking out the door. Nitro was 38 hot that he had to once again get out his bed, just to go feed Angie some dick. Nitro didn't let Mylene know that him and her were recorded that day they were having sex at her father's mansion. Nitro was about to say fuck everything. He had a killer mind and Angie was really pushing him to the edge.

Fifteen minutes later, Nitro was hitting Angie doggy style, watching her ass slap against his skin. Nitro couldn't hold back any longer. He shot a heavy load all over her back. Both were pouring sweat. Angie got out of bed and walked inside her bathroom to clean up. Nitro sat on the edge of the bed going through his phone. He seen he had a missed call from Mylene and Trouble.

Angie came back out the bathroom with a white rag in her hand tossing it to Nitro. "Here clean yourself up. I don't want you to get into trouble," she said with a grin on her face. Nitro took the rag, cleaning himself off before putting his clothes back on.

"I tried calling Trouble to let him know the shipment came in, but he didn't pick up." Angie said stepping into a pair of underwear. It's fifty bricks inside the black bag that's in the living room, sitting in the corner." Nitro knew she was lying about calling Trouble. She just wanted him to stop by and pick up the work himself, so she can get her share as well. Angie was searching through her dresser drawer for a bra. She turned around to see if Nitro was still standing behind her. She realized he was gone. She shook her head at the same time snapping on her bra before walking down the stairs. As soon as Nitro was about to walk out the door with the bag strapped over his shoulder, Angie shouted "Do you still want me to make that call, to get the grass cut," referring to the Marijuana shipment." Nitro turned around to answer Angie's question "Yes, please call and put an order in for three hundred pounds," he said while walking out.

Angie had a smile on her face because she knew that she had Nitro right where she wanted him. In the pussy.

Nitro walked in the house at 9:30 am after dropping off the work to Trouble. He noticed a note on the living room table that read,

"Sorry baby, I couldn't wait long enough for you to come back in. I really thought you would have been back before I went to work but I know you had to take care of your business. I will call you as soon as I get a chance. Your breakfast is in the oven, now let me go, I have a meeting to get to, Love you."

Nitro felt bad that he didn't come back last night. He had got caught up with Angie and left his phone, so he had to circle back to Angie house, then ended up spending the rest of the night with her. Mylene didn't care what Nitro did. She just wanted to be the one to say that's her man.

CHAPTER 21: GOOD OLE' TURK

5:30 pm

THE F.B.I AND SWAT TEAM HAD THE BLOCK OF 34TH STREET and 26th avenue roped off. Turk had laid down the whole Amscott building. Three people had already been shot dead. Turk was already wanted by the Feds for the murder of his girlfriend Shay. He had seven people inside hostage.

"Sir please come out, with your hands up," Agent Gray yelled through a PA horn. Agent Gray radioed in 10-51, meaning to bring in sharp shooters. Turk had two large sacks filled with money in his left hand. The people that were inside were so scared because Turk had already blown one man's head off, right in front of them. Agent Gray received a call on his cellphone.

"Go head Agent Gray speaking; Yes, give me two snipers posted across from the Amscot building, one on top of the Auto Repair Shop and the other on top of the flower Shop. I will draw him to answer the phone again. Once he answers the phone take the shot," Agent Gray ordered before hanging up his phone. Ten minutes later the phone rang inside the building making Turk's heartbeat even faster. Turk kept his eyes and gun on his victims as he eased over towards the phone. The sniper was set up in position waiting for Turk to answer the call. As soon as he picked up the phone the sniper squeezed down on the trigger sending a single slug through the back of his head and exiting out of the front of his forehead, busting his watermelon clean open.

"Man down," Agent Gray yelled out as he watched Turk's head explode through the binoculars, like a firecracker.

CHAPTER 22: BLOODS

NITRO WAS BOBBING HIS HEAD TO THE SOUND OF 2PAC and Snoop Dogg two of Americas most wanted when he was about to turn inside Paradise Apartments. Paradise Apartments is a one way in and one way out. Everyone that lives in the complex are members of the Notorious Blood Gang. If you weren't affiliated with the gang then you were staying inside. You had all ages throwing up the letter B. You even had a couple of old heads sitting out front with red bandannas tied around their necks and wrists playing a game of Dominoes. Nitro pulled his Dodge Viper into the parking lot, he then stepped out the car. That is when he noticed a little boy with a red rag tied around his neck, sitting on a Red Liner bicycle with a pocketknife in his right hand and shirt off, showing his little bird chest.

"What the fuck you doing in here?" the boy said with a mean mug on his face.

"Jit!, You need to put that knife down before you hurt yourself," Nitro said staring at the sharp blade.

"Aye, Lil Red, take your little ass somewhere and play," The slim red-boned girl yelled as she walked towards Nitro, wearing a red wife beater with some cut off white shorts. Showing off her smooth shaved legs. Nitro took a good look at the little boys features before he rode off on his bicycle.

"Why in the fuck you talking to him? And who are you?" she said with a nasty look, wasting no time pulling out her Glock 23 from her waistline.

"Wow, hold up!" Nitro said with his hands up. "I am here to see Phantom, that's all."

"Baby Red, Is there a problem?" A tall, slim, cut up brown-skinned dude said with a red bandanna hanging from his back pocket. Nitro trying to see what she has her gun out for. "You know Two Billy's, if there was a problem, I can handle mine," She replied, pulling out her cellphone making a call. "He say he here to see Phantom," Two Billy's sized Nitro up and then said. "Does Phantom know you're coming through?" "Yeah," Nitro replied

"Aye, do you know about—wait just a minute" as Baby Red cut herself off to ask Nitro his name.

"He says his name is Nitro, that you know about him stopping by. Okay I will let him up," Baby Red said as she hung up with Phantom.

"Follow me," she said with an attitude, tucking her gun back inside her waistline. Nitro walked behind Baby Red watching her ass shift from left to right as she walked up the stairs. Both made it to apartment number B5. She knocked on the door. A short brown-skinned dude with red fire dread tips answered the door, both stepped inside. Nitro quickly took in the décor. He was digging how the place was laid out. A seventy-five-inch big screen television that was attached to the wall with a video game hooked up to it, with two dudes playing a game of Madden. Baby Red asked D-Stylez who was shirtless and sitting on a red leather couch with a dark-skinned girl. "Where is Phantom?' D-Stylez pointed his finger towards the kitchen area then went back to his conversation with the girl. Baby Red and Nitro made their way toward the kitchen where Phantom was watching his brother Burna put the finishing touch on the dope he was whipping up. Phantom had on an all red dickie fit with all red high-top Converses. He had his red bandanna laying over his right shoulder with the dark black Gucci shades sitting on the top of his bald head.

"Phantom," Baby Red shouted out, "your company is here." "What's up big dog? You made it through!" Phantom said, while walking over giving Nitro some dap.

"Homie, Blood don't work for nobody," Phantom said, feeling like Nitro tried him. "Listen Blood, I am not asking you to work for me. All I am saying is cop the work from me and I will make sure you and your people eat good," Nitro replied. "So how much we talkin for a brick?" "Fifteen thousand, only for you," Nitro replied with a serious look. Phantom couldn't help but to jump on that price. He was getting a brick for twenty-one thousand, so saving six thousand is good news to his ears.

"I call that," Phantom said, giving Nitro dap. Nitro knew that Phantom wouldn't turn down that price. Nobody in the city was getting it like him. Straight raw dope off the press, with no cut. Nitro continued to run down the game play to Phantom, letting him know how he will be receiving the drugs.

"Junior get your badass down off that car," Phantom yelled. "Okay uncle," Lil Red replied, climbing down off the car. "So, I guess you know who son that is?" Phantom said with a grin.

"Word, don't tell me, that's Lil Red son? "You already know it is. "Lil bra dropped a seed right before he got killed."

"Man, I had a feeling that was Lil Red jit, he looks just like him. That lil nigga pulled a knife out on me as soon as I stepped out the car," Nitro said with a laugh.

"Homie you got to be kidding me, I just took a knife from him the other day," Phantom said looking down from the balcony watching Lil Red carve 'Billy Gang' into the ground in very big letters.

"Well he got another one back in a heartbeat because he pulled that bitch out on me like it was a gun," Nitro & Phantom both shared a laugh. Nitro looked over at the apartment complex, it was June in the city and the brick building held cold in the winter and heat in the summer. The box fans in lots of the window couldn't be doing much of anything to beat that heat.

The lucky ones had AC units and they were few and far between. It was hot as fuck outside and the temperature had to be at least ten degrees higher or more inside. Most of the residents living there were outside fanning themselves with something as sweat dripped off their bodies and darkened their clothes with sweat on their necks, chest, between their titties and the crack of their asses. You had a couple of dudes shirtless as they balled on the basketball court. You had ladies with a child pressed between their legs as they braided their hair. The kids were ripping and running like they didn't feel the heat from the sun. Now that Phantom scored a cheaper price on the coke tip, he can take care of his people how he wants to.

CHAPTER 23: MORE SECRETS

NITRO HAD MET WITH MYLENE AT A CHINESE restaurant after she got off work, both were seated at a brown table conversing.

"Baby, don't forget that you have to pick up your son this week," Mylene said taking a sip of orange juice from her glass cup.

"I know Bae," he replied.

"Baby, what's wrong?" She asked looking at Nitro, like he wasn't happy to see her. "Nothing bae, I just have a lot going on and Angie is pissing me off," Nitro said as he let Angie's name slip out of his mouth (Angie just called Nitro letting him know that there will be a delay in receiving the marijuana shipment).

"Baby, why you pissed off at Angie? She asked concerned. A Chinese waitress, walked up to Nitro and Mylene's table with the food they ordered. She sat down both plates in front of them and asked. "Would you like a refill of your drinks?" "No ma'am, we are fine, but thank you for asking," Mylene said grabbing a fork, getting ready to dig off in her food.

"Okay, I will be over by the counter. If you need me just wave your hand in the air and I will be here," she said before turning around to go check on the next table.

"Angie just don't listen to nothing I tell her to do at all," Nitro said taking a bite of his baby back ribs. "Baby, Angie always had a problem with listening. When my father got her pregnant and told her to get out the game, she didn't want to listen then either," Mylene said, taking a sip from her drink. Nitro almost choked on his rib bone. The news was a shock to him. No wonder El Mayo spoke English so well. He was curious to know who Angie's baby's father was. Her daughter was real light skinned and Angie's skin complexion was dark, now he knew why Angie was locked in with El Mayo. That's her fucking baby's father, he thought to himself.

"Baby, are you alright? Watch how you eat on that rib you're about to choke yourself."

"I am fine, I just didn't know El Mayo had a baby with Angie," he replied, taking a napkin and wiping around his mouth.

"Baby I can't believe you didn't know that. All this time you been dealing business with my father and you didn't know that."

Now Nitro feels like he can play Angie's little game right along with her. With a smile on his face. Nitro had some fire power now if Angie feels like she wants to drop a little milk, then he will pour all the milk out. Letting El Mayo know that he has been putting the whole ten inches inside Angie.

CHAPTER 24: I PROMISE

TROUBLE WAS JUST LEAVING FROM DROPPING OFF SOME SMOKE to Snow and now on his way to Tameka's house, to surprise her with a ten karat, pink, diamond-cut promise ring.

Tameka was cleaning up the house when she heard a knock on the door. She got a big smile on her face, already knowing who was there.

"Come in, the door is open," she said, as she pushed in her living room chair. Trouble walked inside shaking his head saying to himself, he knew Tameka was in a rich neighborhood because if she was in the hood, she wouldn't be leaving the door unlocked.

"Hey Baby," Tameka said, giving Trouble a kiss on his lips.

"Here, this for you," Trouble said, as he handed Tameka the red roses and balloons.

"Thank you, baby," she said with a big smile on her face. "That's not it, hold tight bae," Trouble said, as he pulled out a small box with a pink ribbon wrapped around it. Tameka was already excited, jumping up and down clapping her hands together like a five-year-old kid that just got her first piece of candy.

"Yes baby, yes baby. I will," she said thinking Trouble had an engagement ring. "Bae, calm down, this is just a promise ring," Trouble said as he watched Tameka's smile ease away.

Trouble read off his own vow "This is a promise ring from me to you. I give you this ring, hoping that you will always remember to stay down, and loyal. Loyalty is everything to me and I hope you will never break that between us. Just know one thing. My love is deep for you and I will do anything to prove my love for you," slipping the ring on Tameka's finger. Tameka's facial expression went right back to a smile.

"Thank you, baby, I love you and you don't have to worry about me breaking your promise." she said, as she kissed Trouble on his lips. Tameka had on a black, silk Dior dress. Trouble squeezed both of Tameka's ass cheeks as both tongue kissed each other down. Trouble whispered in her ear, "You know the boss hate to fight with clothes on." Tameka's smile got even wider. She knew what time it was when Trouble released those words.

"I love this dress on you, but I think it goes better with carpet." Trouble undid her belt and opened her dress, allowing it to fall to her feet. Instantly, Trouble's dick got rock hard.

CHAPTER 25: THAT FLAKA SERIOUS

GUNZ WAS WATCHING A DOPE FIEND BUG OUT IN THE back of his yard, off the new drug called Flaka. "I told that nigga, don't smoke the whole blunt," Gunz said to Big Cookie as they sat back and watched the evil spirit take over the dope fiend's body. "Damn fam, that shit is serious," Big Cookie said to Gunz as he continued to watch as the dope fiend pulled out his twisted hair.

"I know son, this is a real serious drug and once this shit spreads throughout the city, that's when that real paper gonna come in. You just can't do too much because that shit will have you so high on a level that you will not come down," Gunz said with a grin. "Shit, I wouldn't want to be on that type of drug, that shit is for them white boys who like to bug out all the time!" Big Cookie stated.

CHAPTER 26: IT'S OVER

NITRO WAS AT ANGIE'S HOUSE, SITTING ON HER COUCH watching her suck his dick like her life was on the line. Going up and down in a fast motion and making loud slurping sounds. Nitro couldn't hold back the pressure that was building up inside of him. He released a big load of nut inside her mouth. Angie had a little white milk running down the side of her mouth, but the rest went down her throat. Nitro stopped by to let Angie know that her blackmailing days were over with. Angie went inside the bathroom to wash her mouth out. Nitro pulled up his LRG pants and fastened them. Angie came back out the bathroom with a smile on her face.

"What's up, you ready for round two?" she asked, pinning her hair up into a ponytail. "No, I have some business to take care of," Angie's smile erased from her face and she quickly caught an attitude.

"You are not leaving here until I am done with you," Angie replied with her hands on her hips. "Listen Angie, let's get this shit straight. You don't control my dick. My dick controls you. So, this will be the last time you taste this meat in your mouth. Everything from now on is going to be straight business," Nitro said with a dead pen look.

"Nigga you got life fucked up. That is my dick and when I want it, I got it, whenever I feel like it," Angie said with her face balled up.

"Listen Angie, I already told you what it is. You are not getting no more of this meat. I feed you good enough," he replied. "Nigga you got me fucked up," she said, as she walked over and grabbed her cellphone off the glass table, getting ready to make a call.

"Who the fuck you going to call? Your baby's father?" Nitro shouted out, "El Mayo! Make sure he knows that I am putting ten inches of dick down your throat. If you don't, then I will." Nitro said with a grin. Angie eased down the phone from her ear and was surprised to find out that Nitro knew about El Mayo being the father of her daughter. The only one she could think will tell him was Mylene. Now Angie was lost for words because if El Mayo knew that her and Nitro been fucking around behind his back, he will kill her and him. El Mayo did not take kindly to betrayal. El Mayo told Nitro what he will kill for when they first met, and Nitro already knew family was one of them. "Please have that package ready for me this week," Nitro said to Angie before walking out the door with a grin on his face. Angie slammed the door behind him and then balled her fist and punched the door out of anger.

CHAPTER 27: DEADLY

TROUBLE AND TAMEKA WAS LAID UP NEXT TO EACH other talking in bed after two hours of straight rough sex.

"Baby, don't you know that the whole police department was in an uproar about the two detectives getting killed," she said rubbing Trouble's chest.

"Fuck them pigs bae, all them bitches need to die," Trouble said as he smoothly rubbed her arm back and forth. "I know that's right," Tameka said agreeing with Trouble on his comment. Tameka knew Trouble had something to do with the two detectives getting killed.

A few months later the city of St. Petersburg was hit hard with the new drug Flaka. Bayfront Medical Center was filled with patients. The drug was so powerful that people would lose their mind if they used too much. Half the city was taken over as the new drug slowly filled the streets. St. Petersburg city Mayor, Heller, was downtown at City Hall making a public announcement about the deadly drug. He was informing news reporters of how he will handle the situation.

"Mr. Heller, do you know when the drug Flaka first hit the city?" A slim white reporter asked, as he held up his tape recorder, making sure he got everything that was being said. "Yes," Mayor Heller replied. "So why did you wait so late to move in on the deadly drug?"

"Next question please," Mayor Heller said moving on to the next reporter. He felt like he didn't have to answer that question because he knew that he didn't move efficiently when the drug first hit the city.

"Mr. Mayor, how are you planning on fighting the new drug?" A skinny blonde asked.

"Right now, a drug task force unit is being put together as we speak. I talked with the St. Petersburg Police Department Chief. Once everything is put together, the unit will tackle the streets."

Trouble and Nitro were sitting at the spot watching the news press.

"Bra this shit is slowing down our paper for real. The fiends don't even want crack anymore, they're asking for that Flaka shit now." Trouble said, counting a couple of Benjamin's in his hand.

"Did you talk with Angie about finding the new drug?" "Angie said, that she talked with El Mayo about the Flaka drug, but he didn't know what she was talking about," Nitro replied.

"Bra tell me this, who you think pushing that shit through the City?" Trouble asked, while splitting a blunt down the middle and then dumping out the guts.

"I got word from Angie and she was saying that one of her girlfriends talk to this nigga who supposed to be pushing it. A nigga named Gunz from New York. Angie said that she was going to get back with me on that tip."

"I hope she do because you already know kid, about that paper, we ready to go to war," Trouble said pulling out his Glock 40 and placing it on his lap. Nitro had a grin on his face because he knew Trouble didn't even fuck off when it came to his paper. He felt the same way, if you weren't a part of the team then you were an enemy.

CHAPTER 28: FINALLY SET FREE

Nitro pulled up in front of Martin Correctional Institution in a dark tinted, stretch Hummer, to pick up his father. The two-hundred-and-fifty-pound straight muscle bound, Michael Knight Sr., stepped out the gates wearing a black and gray Burberry suit, with the matching gators, like he owned some successful businesses. Nitro had shipped off his father's release clothes through first class mail, so when he stepped out the gate, he will be clean as a whistle. Nitro had a Big Smile on his face, happy to see that his father being released from the prison walls. He told his father to tell them boys that are behind the G-walls to look out their window when he gets EOS, so they can see how big his father riding. Nitro's father did exactly what his son told him to do. He had every inmate who can see the parking lot from their cell windows. Some were even yelling out the windows making the captain come out on the scene.

"Welcome home Pops," Nitro said giving his father a big hug. "Thanks son, I am proud to be out," his father replied, squeezing Nitro tight like that was his last hug.

"I have a surprise for you," Nitro said. "And what would that be?" His father replied. Nitro gave Big Joe a head nod and seconds later Big Joe opened the back door showing off five beautiful women of all different races.

"Have any one of them. You have five different flavors. Try them all if you want," Nitro said as he watched his father's tongue hang out his mouth like a dog in heat. Nitro knew that his father hasn't had any pussy in decades. Both hopped into the backseat then took off. Their first stop was a five-star restaurant. Nitro's father hadn't had any good cooking in years. He was used to eating that watered-down slop they served in prison. He didn't know what real food tasted like. After several hours of shopping, Nitro decided to take GMC out to celebrate.

It was Friday night at Club Luxury. Nitro's clique pulled up in front of the club in three stretch Hummers back to back. Everyone that he was with him entered the building Iced out, even the females. Nitro had his father set up inside a private room with three exotic dancers that were giving him the best time of his life. Trouble was in the VIP section with the rest of GMC, balling out of control. Pouring Cristal and smoking on the best weed, money can buy. Nitro peeked inside the room and saw his father getting his dick sucked by three girls. Nitro gave his father thumbs up, before heading back to the VIP section.

CHAPTER 29: THE HOT HOUSE

IT WAS 1:30 AM AND DENISE WAS PUTTING THE LAST THREE bottles of Armadale Vodka up. She then walked over to her kitchen table to count the money she made for the night.

Denise never went out to the club on a Friday night. She always stayed back and sold liqueur to the ones that didn't go out to the club. Denise ran her hot house every time she got off work. If Ike made her stay overtime at the store. She will have her girlfriend Ebony run the house until she got off work. Denise heard four knocks at the door, she got up out of her seat without grabbing her gun and looked out her kitchen window. She noticed Ebony standing before her eyes, with her purse strapped over her shoulder.

"Ebony, why in the hell weren't you answering the phone?" Denise said loudly before she opened her door. Ray and Chucky, shoved Ebony inside the house, knocking Denise down onto the kitchen floor. Both had guns drawn out demanding to know where the money was. Ray and Chucky ran down on Ebony at the gas station, forced her inside the car with a gun to her head and made her drive to the house.

"Bitch, get your ass up and show me where the money is," Chucky said as he slapped Denise across her head with the butt of his gun, making blood pour down her forehead. Ray grabbed Ebony and hog-tied her, sticking a dirty sock inside her mouth. Chucky grabbed Denise by her neck putting the barrel of his gun inside her mouth.

"Ima ask you one last time, where's the money? Chucky asked. "In the bedroom," Denise mumbles with tears racing down her face. "Let's go," Chucky replied before grabbing eight hundred dollars off the Kitchen table, from what Denise made for that night, then stuffing it inside his pocket.

Chucky pushed Denise inside the bedroom giving her one more good strike across the head, she fell to the floor. "Get up Bitch, and get what I came for," Chucky said with his gun pointed at Denise's face. She got up off the floor, and quickly made her way to her bedroom closet. Denise grabbed two boxes filled with money, and then handed it to Chucky. Chucky opened the shoe box and saw 10's, 20's, 50's, 100's, his eyes turned straight into dollar signs. Chucky looked at Denise wearing black, tight, skinny jeans, showing off all her gorgeous curves. Denise had that exotic look, so her beauty stood out. Chucky walked up close to her, lifting her chin up with the barrel of his gun looking her straight in the eyes with lust.

"Them clothes look sexy on you, but I think they will look even better off," Chucky said in a low tone of voice.

"No, Please," Denise said shaking her head from left to right.

"Please no, I gave you all the money please don't rape me," she said pleading for Chucky not to rape her.

"Baby just do what I say, and I will not hurt you," he said sticking his tongue out and licking her on the face. Denise trembled when she felt his moist tongue. "Now come out of them clothes" he ordered as he sat both shoeboxes down on the floor. He then pulled out a magnum condom from his back pocket. Denise didn't want to comply to the order that was given to her, but she didn't have a choice. She would either do what she was told, or he would kill her, she thought.

Chucky dick went from soft to hard as he watched Denise take off her bra and panties. Her breasts were the perfect size and her skin was flawless. Chucky slipped on the condom and told Denise to lay down on the bed. Chucky got between her legs and threw them both on top of his shoulders before digging off inside of her. He pumped away as he looked down into Denise's watery eyes, telling her to stop with the crying because he couldn't concentrate. She could not stop the tears from coming down her face, she couldn't believe that she was getting raped.

"Bitch didn't I tell you to stop with that mutha fuckin crying," Chucky yelled as he slapped Denise in her mouth, causing her bottom lip to bleed. After he got his nut, he pulled out of her, snatched the condom off and tossed it to the side. Denise was shocked and frightened, she didn't know what Chucky would do next.

"I am sorry, I can't stop crying," she said with her arms crossed over her breasts.

"Bitch you don't have to worry about crying anymore," he said pulling out his gun from his pocket. Denise's eyes grew bigger when she saw the gun in his hand. Chucky let off four shots into Denise's chest, turning her white sheets to red, as she lay in her own pool of blood. Chucky grabbed the shoeboxes from off the floor and made his way back toward the kitchen where he noticed Ebony laying with a small hole in the middle of her forehead, her clothes were torn apart and panties off. Chucky could easily tell that Ray had took the pussy.

"Damn Nigga, what took you so long?" Ray asked as he fastened his belt buckle.

"Nigga the hoe was playing games when telling me where the money was, but I got it and then put a bullet in the hoe head for playing games," Chucky said lying to his partner in crime. Ray already knew that Chucky was lying to him because he heard moaning coming from inside the bedroom when he walked up to the door,

"Yeah, whatever Nigga. Let's get the fuck out of here," Ray said, as he peeked out the window before walking out the door.

CHAPTER 30: THE DAY AFTER

IT WAS THREE IN THE MORNING AND CLUB LUXURY WAS closing. Nitro and Mylene exited the club, straight into the back seat of a stretch Hummer that was waiting out front. Mylene was upset with Nitro, because his phone kept lighting up while they were inside the club. The only thing Mylene could think was that another chick was texting his phone.

"So, you not going to tell me who was texting your phone at three in the morning? Mylene asked with her arms crossed over each other.

"Listen Mylene, I told you that wasn't nobody," Nitro replied.

"That's bullshit Nitro. I am not going to be played like one of these little hoes out here," Mylene loudly said as she watched Nitro pour the red wine into two glass cups.

"Look Mylene," he said as he put the glass bottle down and slid over next to her. He put his hand under her short black Chanel dress, moved her thong to the side and stuck his middle finger inside her pussy, making her become instantly wet.

Mylene closed her eyes and bit down on her bottom lip. She was already feeling tipsy and high from the back to back weed smoking.

"Damn baby, that feels so good," she said as she accepted Nitro's finger. Nitro had a grin on his face. He slipped his finger in and out of her wet box. He knew exactly how to get Mylene's mind off the cheating stuff. Mylene spread her legs wider so he can get deep inside her. Nitro pulled his wet finger out of her pussy for a minute, to take off his clothes. He pulled down his pants and pinned Mylene to the seat and went straight to work.

The Following Day

Tameka woke up with breakfast in bed. After a long night with Trouble partying all night, celebrating Nitro's father release from prison. When they got back to the house it was like a race to see who can be the first one out of their clothes. Trouble was standing right before Tameka's eyes with a white robe on and a silver food trey in his hands. He had cheese grits, bacon, eggs with chopped green peppers, butter milk biscuits and a glass of orange juice. Tameka had a big smile on her face. No one ever brought her breakfast in bed. Trouble was the first to do that.

"I figure since you took me on a long ride last night and you might be a little tired, I would take over the kitchen this morning," Trouble said, handing Tameka the tray.

"Thank you, baby." Tameka thought Trouble had hit it right on the head. She didn't feel like getting up for anything. It was her day off, so she wanted to enjoy her time with Trouble.

She took a bite into her butter milk biscuit when she heard her phone ring. Trouble looked over on the nightstand and thought to himself, who could be calling so early in the morning? "Baby, can you hand me that?" she said with a strange look on her face, as well wondering who is calling. Tameka answered her phone in a low tone voice.

"Hello," she said as she put down her biscuit. Trouble stood by and waited to see who was on the other side of the line. By the change of look on Tameka's face, he knew that it wasn't good. "Come on Morgan, this is my day off. You don't have anyone else that can go out," Tameka said with a puppy face. "Okay, I will be there, give me 35 minutes to get myself together," she said before hanging up.

"Baby, I got to go to work. These mutha fuckers are calling me when it's my day off. Damn, I can't relax," Tameka got out her bed with a gray see through thong on. She walked up to Trouble and put her arms around his neck.

"Baby, I am so mad right now," she said, giving Trouble a kiss. "Don't worry bae, we will have time to hang out," he replied looking Tameka in her beautiful eyes.

"Baby, I got thirty-five minutes to get ready for work, so let's get a quickie in," she said grabbing Troubles dick. "Look at you. You just can't wait for daddy's dick," Trouble replied with a grin.

"Nope, I can't wait, so come get this pussy and make me cum hard." Tameka pulled down her panties and bent over the bed. Trouble loosened his robe belt and then fell inside Tameka's wet pussy.

CHAPTER 31: I'M OUT!

NITRO WAS SITTING OVER AT EL MAYO'S PLACE, HIM AND another bonafide hustler that goes by the name Ghost. Ghost was another one of El Mayo's soldiers who played on his team. All three were having a drink and discussing business. Nitro bumped into Ghost a couple of times, but never minded what him and El Mayo had going on. He was always there for his business only.

"Listen El Mayo, no disrespect but I am not giving up Louisiana. I built that from the ground up. I am the one that had soldiers in the battlefield, dropping down anyone who didn't want to fall in line," Nitro said as he stood up patting his chest. Now you're telling me that you want someone else to take over?" he said with a dead pen look.

"Listen El Mayo, I am out, I don't have time to keep rebuilding the city like I am some goddamn construction worker or something. I put work on every block inside New Orleans, now you're telling me that you want someone else to take over. Someone that don't grind harder than me or my clique," Nitro said in a loud hostile voice. Nitro picked up his jacket from the chair and made his way to the front door. Nitro didn't care if El Mayo sold him another brick ever again. He made enough money that he could buy his own poppy plant farm now. Ghost had a grin on his face, thinking to himself that he can get Nitro out the Circle for good.

CHAPTER 32: MY NIECE

TAMEKA PULLED UP ON THE BLOCK OF 22ND AVENUE and 14th street south in her smoke gray Mercedes Benz. She didn't have time to go to the station and switch vehicles. Tameka stepped out of her car throwing her gold badge around her neck, then walked up to the crime scene.

"Good morning Ms. Foster," A tall, slim built officer said while holding up the yellow tape for her to cross under.

"Good morning to you officer SIK, she replied. What do we have here?" She asked SIK, looking him directly in his eyes.

"We have two dead, one in the kitchen, and the other one in the bedroom. Both are females. Looks like they are in their late twenties," Officer SIK said as they both stepped inside.

"Both girls have been raped and shot." Tameka took a knee down, checking out the dried-up blood that covered the girls face. Tameka noticed the small hole in the middle of the girl's forehead. You had three officers already inside the house taking pictures and dusting for fingerprints.

"We retrieved two condoms, both had semen inside them. I sent it to the lab for DNA samples. These stupid mother fuckers didn't take the time to get rid of the evidence," officer SIK said, with a grin on his face. He suspected two suspects since they found a different condom on the bedroom floor. Tameka stood up and looked over the girl's bloody body and saw her underwear were torn and thrown to the side. She then kneed back down to pick the underwear up with her Ink Pen.

"Make sure you get all evidence, don't miss anything," She said as a white heavy-set officer walked up to her with a brown bag.

"From the look of things, the person that's staying here was selling illegal alcohol," officer SIK said as he opened the bedroom door. Tameka witnessed Denise stretched out across the bed with four gunshot wounds to her chest.

"Oh my God. Denise how could this happen?" she asked herself with one hand cover her mouth. Denise was Tameka's niece from her oldest sister. She was lost for words, trying to figure out how she was going to explain Denise's death to her sister. Tameka didn't know that Denise involved herself with criminal activity. She always thought that Denise was the princess of the family. Tameka's sister worked very hard every day as a single mother to put clothes on her daughters back, now Tameka doesn't know how to tell her sister that her only daughter is dead.

Denise's body was carried out of the house on a stretcher, zipped inside a black bag while Tameka was standing out front with tears running down her face, as she watched the emergency assistant put her niece's body inside the ambulance. She pulled her phone out and made a call to her sister.

"Hey sis, where are you right now? Okay, stay right there. I will be there in 20 minutes," she said as she hung up the phone. "Are you going to be alright?" Officer SIK asked rubbing her back. "Yes, I will. Thank you," She replied back emotionally.

Tameka pulled up in front of New Mount Olive Primitive Baptism Church. The church was just letting out from service. Tameka spotted her sister walking out into the parking lot. She turned inside to catch her before she got inside her car. Tameka quickly parked in an open space and exited her car.

"ERICA." Tameka shouted out. Erica and her friend were walking when they turned around to see who could be shouting Erica's name. "Hey baby girl. I was just about to call you when I got inside my car," Erica said. Tameka felt a little at ease when she saw Erica's best friend Tushawn. She knew Tushawn would be there to support her when she broke down.

"Step to the side for a minute, I got something I need to tell you," Tameka said getting ready to give her sister the sad news.

"Excuse me for a minute, Tushawn. Can you please take this back to the car for me," Erica asked giving Tushawn her keys and her purse. "Sure," Tushawn replied.

Erica & Tameka was left alone as Tushawn took Erika's things back to the car.

"What's up baby girl, what's going on?

"Listen Erica I don't know how I am going to tell you this, but I have to. Something happened overnight at Denise's home. Officers got a call to Denise's address and when the officers arrived, they found Denise dead along with another girl inside the home." Tameka stood and watched her sister's smile turn into a frown.

"NO, NO, NO, Noooooooo... Please God NO. Erica fell into Tameka arms pouring tears. Tameka comforted her sister as much as she could until Tushawn pulled up with the car.

CHAPTER 33: LET'S MEET GUNZ

"**F**UCK THAT SHIT EATING MUTHA FUCKA. I FEEL LIKE we need to touch his ass anyways," Trouble bawled out while removing his 9mm bullets from his clip, replacing them with hollow points.

"Don't worry bra, I have a plan on what we're going to do," Nitro said rolling up a blunt.

"Oh yeah? I got off the phone with Angie a couple minutes ago, she was trying to hit your line to let you know about that Nigga named Gunz from NYC. He has a restaurant on central avenue called The Hot Spot," Trouble said reaching for the blunt out of Nitro's hand.

"Okay. Hit up the Pirate kids and the rest of the clique and tell them to meet us at the spot. Let's pay Gunz a first-time visit," Nitro said, pulling out his Glock 40 and checking his clip to see how many bullets he was holding.

GMC pulled up in front of Gunz's restaurant seven cars deep. Everyone stepped out and walked inside. Gunz was seated at a table with a couple of his hit squad crew, when he noticed a large group of people mobbing inside wearing all black. Big Cookie stood up in position as well as NYC, clutching on her strap inside her Prada purse.

"I need to speak with Gunz and I am not leaving until I do so," Nitro said with a straight face.

"For what reason?" Gunz asked, playing like he wasn't the person Nitro asked for.

"Motha fucka, I don't need for you to be asking me any questions. I told you who I need to talk with," Nitro said. Big Cookie and the other hit squad members drew their guns and Nitro and GMC pulled out their weapons as well. Both sides had guns pointed at each other's faces.

"Hold up, wait a minute, this is not good for business," Gunz said with his arms stretched out telling both sides to put down their weapons. GMC weren't following any orders if they weren't coming from their boss. Nitro let his Clique know to ease down their weapons. Angie and NYC were face to face after they put down they guns. A couple of people that were still inside the restaurant quickly rushed out the front door.

"Let's talk son, follow me this way," Gunz said. Nitro told his team to stand by while he goes in the back and talks with Gunz.

CHAPTER 34: BABY PHAT

"**P**USSY ASS HOE, GET YOUR SHIT AND GET THE FUCK OUT of my house. Hoe, you didn't think I would catch on and find out that you were stealing my money. After all the shit I did for you. Slap!" Baby Phat hit her best friend Courtney across the face with her gun in hand and cut her on the cheek bone, making her leak blood everywhere. Courtney balled up in a frightened position in the corner of Baby Phat's bedroom.

"I want my twenty thousand dollars back," Baby Phat cried out before letting off a single shot into Courtney's thigh. Courtney screamed out from the burning hot bullet.

"Okay Baby Phat, I will get the money back," Courtney said, crying and holding her thigh at the same time, trying to stop the blood.

CHAPTER 35: THE CONSENSUS

"**S**O, YOU'RE SAYING THAT YOU WILL PUT UP A MILLION dollars and we will both have dealing on moving the drugs from state to state?"

"Yes, Nitro replied. With your soldiers and mine. Nothing will be able to stop us." Nitro said looking at Gunz rub his red nose Pit Bull.

"Okay we can make that happen I'm in. Let's get this money," Gunz said with a grin, giving Nitro some dap. Just like that the two had joined forces.

Nitro stepped inside the house at eight thirty at night where he witnessed Mylene sitting on the couch crying. Nitro dropped his Gucci bag that had thirty-two thousand dollars inside and quickly rushed to her side, to see what was wrong.

"Baby what's wrong?" Nitro asked. "I just had a big fight with my father over the phone,"

She said in between catching her breath. "He said that he seen a tape with us having sex." Nitro was disappointed to hear Mylene tell him that. He thought that him and Angie had an understanding and that she would not let El Mayo know he was sexing his daughter.

"Baby he told me that I can't be with you and that you're no longer in the family. I let him know that I am not leaving you," Mylene said looking up into Nitro eyes. "Don't worry bae. Your father is not going to stop us from being together," Nitro said as his blood started boiling for Angie. Nitro was 38 hot.

"He said that I can die right along with you because I am not showing any type of loyalty to the family by not following his orders." "Listen to me bae, look at me," he said, lifting her chin up. "I am not going to let anything happen to you." He reached under the couch and pulled out an AR-15 assault rifle. He handed the powerful weapon to her and said "Bae, all you have to do is squeeze down on the trigger. If you see anything that's not me." Mylene held the heavy weapon in her hand and nodded her head.

"I will be right back. I got to go take care of some business," Nitro stood up and quickly rushed into the bedroom to throw on a black tee with the matching skullcap. Nitro pulled open his top dresser drawer and grabbed his chrome Desert Eagle with the clip that was beside it. He then jammed the clip inside the gun and cocked the hummer back, making Mylene quickly turn her head towards the bedroom when she heard the loud sound. Nitro tucked his gun underneath his shirt, then came out of the bedroom in a fast pace.

"Bae I will be back," he said before giving Mylene a kiss on the lips. "Be careful." she replied, as she watched Nitro walk out the door.

Angie was home sitting on her couch watching a movie and eating a bag of popcorn when she heard three loud knocks at her door. She got up to see who it could be "Wait just a minute." She said as she walked towards the front door. She looked through her peep hole and noticed Nitro standing out front. "Nitro, boy, why in the hell are you knocking on my door so mutha fuckin hard? Like you're the police or something" she asked as she opened the door. Angie had a smile on her face once she saw who it was. On the other hand, Nitro wasn't for all the smiles. He slapped the shit out of Angie sending her flying to the ground.

"You just couldn't keep your mouth closed bitch," Nitro shouted. Angie's bottom lip was dripping blood as she watched Nitro step her way.

"Nigga, what the fuck are you talking about?" she bawled out. "Bitch, you know what the fuck I am talking about. Bitch stop playing stupid and tell me how in the fuck El Mayo seen the video?" he yelled with an evil look on his face.

"Nitro I don't know what the fuck you're talking about." Angie replied, afraid of what Nitro was going to do next.

"Bitch I knew that me and you weren't going to last long," Nitro said before he squeezed down on the trigger sending four slugs into Angie's chest. Nitro Scrambled through the house making sure no one else was inside before he slid out of the door.

CHAPTER 36: LOYALTY OVER EVERYTHING

EL MAYO WAS SITTING INSIDE HIS OFFICE IN A LAZY BOY chair with both of his feet kicked up on his desk watching two, top of the line models/strippers take off their clothes. El Mayo's assistant got both girls out of a Miami club called K.O.D, meaning King of Diamonds. After seeing how beautiful both girls were, El Mayo told them both that they don't have to ever go back stripping for the club again. That they can be his own private dancers. El Mayo took sight of Ghost walking down his hallway on his security camera's he had set up throughout his home. Before Ghost could even get a chance to knock on the door, he was welcomed inside by a brown skinned female with dark brown eyes. Wearing an all-white G-string. Ghost walked inside El Mayo's office with his game face on. Ready to be the next big thing smoking. He knew by showing El Mayo the tape that he would get Nitro kicked out of the family for good. Ghost stood by and watched El Mayo run his nose across the mountain of cocaine that was laid out across his desk. El Mayo jumped out of his seat and did a three sixty after sniffing up the cocaine.

"That's what I am talking about. That white girl is a bitch," he cried out in his Spanish accent. El Mayo cut down the volume on his remote to his built-in stereo system and told both girls to get out. With no time wasting, both girls picked up their belongings and rushed out of the door.

Ghost loved when he walked into El Mayo's office. He had the same set-up that Tony Montana had on the movie Scar Face.

"You are welcome my friend, help yourself." El Mayo said pointing his finger at the cocaine, letting him know that he can take a line himself.

Ghost shook his head telling El Mayo no thank you. Sniffing cocaine wasn't Ghosts thing. Smoking marijuana always took a toll on his life. Ghost stopped by to give El Mayo the latest update on his daughter's words and what she told him.

"So, did you hear from my daughter?" El Mayo asked as he sat down in his chair.

"Yes, I did. She said that she wasn't going to leave him alone," Ghost said as he stood and watched the expression on El Mayo's face. Well, I guess she can die too," El Mayo said as he sniffed a straight line of the coke. "Mr. EL Mayo, are you sure about that, because….." Before Ghost could finish his sentence El Mayo quickly jumped out of his seat and went to fussing. Ghost knew when El Mayo gets to speaking in Spanish, there's a problem.

"Listen to me Ghost, my friend, kill them both and bring me back their heads," El Mayo said, feeling like his head was about to explode from sniffing too much coke.

"Yes Sir, I will handle that." What Ghost realized about El Mayo is that he didn't fuck off when it comes to family and loyalty. If he felt like you betrayed the family in any type of way, off goes your head. Ghost never thought it would turn out to be so serious that El Mayo would send a hit on his own daughter.

"Take Ms. Kimbella with you. She is a professional killer," El Mayo said as he picked up the roll of hundred-dollar bills and took another straight line of coke up his nose. Kimbella stepped out of the jacuzzi dripping wet wearing a yellow one-piece bathing suit. She had exotic features. Light green eyes, caramel skin complexion, with long jet-black silky hair, that hung down the middle of her back. Her 36-29-41 body of a goddess will have a man craving for it. Ghost could easily tell that she had work done to her body. Her breast stood straight up at attention. Ghost straightened his eyes and took his mind off lust and got back to business.

"I will not have a problem with her assisting me," Ghost said looking straight at Kimbella as she blinked her right eye at him.

The following day Nitro had his whole GMC at the round table discussing the issue with him and El Mayo. "Right now, we are at war with this wet back," Nitro stated.

"GMC don't kiss nobody's ass and we damn sure ain't going to start or back down from no one," Trouble said with a deadpan look. "As you can see, Angie is no longer with us." Nitro said as he looked around the table and seen that everyone had a strange look upon their faces.

"I need for everyone to be on point, because you never know when this wetback will strike." Nitro said as he fired up a blunt and inhaled the weed smoke. "I already put Gunz and his hit squad crew on point, so they're ready as well. Everyone was still waiting to see what was up with Angie, but Nitro never made it back around to that topic and nobody bothered to ask.

"We will have two extra soldiers posted up on each end of the street with walkie-talkies. Every time a car rides down any street or near where we are, it will be radioed in. We can't get caught slippin," Nitro said while blowing out a white cloud of smoke from his mouth.

After an hour of talking and letting the team know that they're at war, Nitro and Trouble stepped off to the side and had a small conversation amongst each other.

"Listen Nitro, don't be worrying about that wetback. If he was going to make a move he would have done it by now. He's just barking, not biting." Trouble said with his right hand on Nitro's shoulder. Nitro didn't put anything past El Mayo. He knew that he could cause damage and he didn't want to get caught slipping. "Listen Big bra, let's go hang out and get your mind off that shit. If he comes our way, we'll deal with him accordingly," Trouble said with a serious look. Nitro really wasn't worried about his safety. His main worry was Mylene's safety. "I will be to pick you up at 1:30 so be ready and I am not taking no for an answer," Trouble said before walking out of the door. Nitro didn't feel like doing any partying because he knew that he was at war. But he didn't want to leave his friend hanging so he made the choice of stepping out with Trouble to the club in full gear.

Hours later, Club Level was jam packed. Everyone came out for Lil' Boosie's welcome home bash. The huge parking lot was filled to capacity, as cars continued to pile in. Nitro and Trouble was stationed at the bar, surrounded by a crowd of girls. Before they entered the club, Trouble let Nitro know that he has a child on the way. That put a smile on Nitro's face to hear that his friends are bringing a little one into the world. Nitro had bought the bar out letting his partner know that they will be celebrating until lights out. What Nitro and Trouble didn't know was that the enemy was already placed inside the club in position.

Two hours later a fight broke out, and shots begin to ring out. Nitro & Trouble exit through the backdoor of the club where Trouble's black Lexus was parked. Trouble and Nitro jumped into the front seat and a brown skinned young lady that Trouble met in the club hopped in the back seat.

"Bra, did you see what happened? Trouble asked nearly out of breath from the running he did out the club, "That Nigga who got hit with the bottle, his..." Before Trouble could finish his sentence, the girl reached into her garter belt and pulled out a Snub-Nosed 22 Pistol. She let off one single shot to the back of Troubles head and then reached over and shot Nitro three times to the chest. Trouble's limp head rested on his steering wheel, causing his horn to blow continuously. Blood covered the front window.

Kimbella smiled. She loved what she did because she was damn good at it. She was one of the most prolific hit-hoes (as in hitman) in the underground world. She could get the job done quicker than anyone that El Mayo ever hired as a hitman. She looked at Nitro as he took his last breath and closed his eyes. Just as she was about to step out of the car to meet up with Ghost in the front, as he had instructed her earlier, a phone rang. It was Nitro's cell.

"Hello?" Kimbella said, trying to add salt to the wound. She always did messy things like that. She got an adrenaline rush and laughter out of her bold sinister humor. "Who is this? Where is Nitro?" Mylene asked.

"He's sleeping," Kimbella replied before letting out a big laugh and hanging up. She left the car, leaving Trouble and Nitro slumped. Mylene was dumb founded. She just looked at her phone in disbelief, her heart crumbled at the fact that another woman had picked up Nitro's phone. Nitro already called Mylene and told her once he left the Club that he would be coming straight home. Yet, now Mylene was hurt to even imagine Nitro being with another woman after she gave up everything to be with him.

El Mayo was sitting inside his custom design movie theater in his home with a black and Chinese female. "El Mayo Sir, phone is for you," the bald-head, Spanish security guard said as he handed El Mayo the phone. On the other end of the line was Ghost calling, letting El Mayo know that the job was taken care of and that his daughter wasn't nowhere around. After hearing what Ghost had to say, El Mayo pressed one number on his phone, letting Ghost know that he heard everything before he disconnected the call. He then turned his head toward the woman he was sitting next to and blew a thick cloud of smoke in her face. The beautiful girl grinned before she turned her head back to finish watching a Kung Fu movie. El Mayo never held a conversation over the phone. He felt like the Feds had his phone tapped. He told himself that he wouldn't ever give them a chance to railroad him. He knew how the Feds moved and operated after putting you under surveillance.

El Mayo reached inside his top shirt pocket and pulled out a small gold case that had Christina Aguilera inside. He then opened it and took his rolled up one-hundred-dollar bill from behind his ear and swiped it across the glass mirror twice, sniffing the cocaine before passing it off to the girl. He leaned deep into his seat as he felt the high hit his body like a ton of bricks. The girl snorted the rest of the coke, leaving nothing on the glass. She took it up her nose like a straight champ. El Mayo had a boss like grin on his face as he sat slumped down in his seat, high from the cocaine, thinking how his daughter will be mourning the death of Nitro once she hears the news.

Nitro woke up with an aching pain in his chest. He looked over to his left and saw his partner slumped on the steering wheel. It all happened so fast that Nitro couldn't believe it.

"Trouble," Nitro whispered. He tried to shake him but to no avail. Trouble was already gone. The bullet-proof vest Nitro was wearing protected him from the bullets that Kimbella shot. There was still a nagging pain in his shoulder that wouldn't go away.

"Trouble!" Nitro managed to scream as he continued to shake him. He couldn't grasp the reality. Shock took over his reactions as he tried his hardest to wake Trouble. Blood trickled onto Nitro's hand, that's when he noticed the small hole in the back of Trouble's head. Seeing his right-hand man with a hole in the back of his head was too much to bear. Nitro let out a painful roar as tears welled up in his eyes and his vision began to blur. Nitro heard sirens and looked in the rearview mirror. He reached for the door; an intense pain shot through his body.

"Ahh shit," he yelled out. He stumbled out of the car and for the first time he noticed all the blood on his own shirt. He patted his body frantically to see where he was hit. He was in shock and couldn't pinpoint where the pain in his body was coming from. An ambulance and police cars pulled up simultaneously as Nitro fell to his knees.

"Put your hands up where I can see them!" the police called.

"It aint me! They got Trouble in the car," he muttered as he held his body up by placing one hand on the ground.

"Help Trouble!" Nitro shouted as he began to cough up blood. The Paramedics rushed over to him and immediately began work. "We have a bullet wound to the shoulder. Get me some oxygen and let's start an IV." The medic called out to his peers. Nitro felt weak and the taste of blood in his mouth frightened him. "We're going to have to question him," one of the Officers stated.

"You're going to have to wait until he gets this bullet removed. If not, he's going to bleed to death." The medic stated sternly as he helped place Nitro's body on a stretcher. Nitro was slipping in and out of consciousness and was losing pints of blood. As Nitro's head fell to the side, he witnessed the police zip up Trouble's body bag.

"Trouble," he whispered faintly. Anger ripped through Nitro.

Nitro was so close to Trouble that it hurt him to see his friend that he knew since middle school, leave from by his side. He and Trouble did everything together, from busting licks to making money and fucking hoes. Now he had to say farewell to his partner in crime. Nitro knew that there was only one person who would be so bold to attempt a hit on his life. He knew exactly who was behind the hit. Nitro promised himself that he was going to make El Mayo pay with his life.

Mylene sat by the window, staring blankly at the stars into the night sky. Letting her hair blow freely through the wind, her heart aching at the fact that Nitro was with another girl. She couldn't help it though, she didn't care if he had a thousand other girls, she had to be a part of his life. Her heart beat rapidly as she impatiently waited for Nitro to come home. She was furious with him, but she needed him. Where is he? She thought solemnly as tears fell from her face. Her anxiety was eating her up inside. Every time a car rode down her street, she would go to the window and look out, hoping it would be Nitro pulling up. "Why isn't he here?" she asked aloud. "He's probably fucking with some bitch." She checked the clock on the wall and noticed that it read 4:30 am. He was supposed to have been home an hour ago. Her mind was telling her to give up and pack her things, but her heart wouldn't allow her to. Mylene sat in front of the window until dusk turned to dawn and the night life gave way to the bright sunlight.

"What have I done? She asked herself as she finally came to terms with her reality. She had hoped that things would go back to normal and her father would just accept the fact that she loved Nitro.

Ring! Ring! The screeching blare of the telephone startled her, and she staggered to her feet to answer it. She silently wished it to be Nitro. She wiped her eyes and nose as she tried to calm down before picking up the phone.

"Hello?" she stated, her voice cracking in her attempt to sound okay. "Hey Mylene, this Big Joe. Nitro and Trouble been shot! I am on my way to pick you up," Big Joe said in a high tone of voice.

"Oh my God. Hurry I am ready." She said in shock. "They got shot at the club. The nurse wouldn't tell me anything over the phone. "What hospital are they at?" "Tampa General," Big Joe replied. "I am out front come out." Mylene hung up her phone without saying another word and rushed out the door.

Twenty-five minutes later, Mylene & Big Joe were at the hospital trying to get some information about Nitro and Trouble's whereabouts. Trouble's sister Reecee rushed inside the hospital as she got a call from one of the doctors letting her know that her brother had been shot. Mylene, Reecee and Big Joe stood in front of the nurse's desk, impatiently waiting to receive news on Nitro and Trouble's condition.

"Is he okay?" Mylene asked. When she didn't get an immediate response, she yelled in frustration. "Why won't you tell me anything!?" "You really should wait for the doctor," the nurse told her.

"He will help you understand what happened." "Fuck you mean?" Reecee stated in exasperation. "Understand what? What happened? Please just tell us that they're okay."

"I'm sorry, Miss. I can't," the nurse replied. Reecee knocked all of the nurse's papers off the counter and stormed out of the hospital in a pained rage. Her head felt like it was going to explode. I need to get some fresh air, she thought, as she rushed out of the double doors that led to the emergency room parking lot. Just as Reecee was about to sit down on the curb, she saw Mylene running toward her with Big Joe right behind. Mylene hugged Reecee tightly as she watched tears pour from her eyes. "What happened, Mylene? Where is my brother?" Reecee was concerned as she sobbed in her arms. "I don't know Reecee. They ain't telling me shit. Everything is gone be alright." Mylene said unconvincingly. "Come on, it's too cold to be standing out here. Let's wait inside." Mylene and Reecee made it back to the waiting room, where they both sat solemnly in silence, consumed with their own thoughts.

It was now almost noon. Ten hours had passed since Nitro & Trouble had been shot. Reecee was in the hospital waiting on the outcome, yet she was still in the dark about her brother's status. She was more than thankful that Trouble had her name listed under sister in the address portion of his iPhone.

That was the only way that the doctors were able to contact her to inform her that her brother had been shot.

But now the unending wait to find out his condition was like torture. Another hour passed before a doctor finally came out to see them.

"How is my brother? Reecee asked as soon as she saw the doctor step into the room.

"I apologize for keeping you waiting this long." the doctor stated. "I don't want to have to tell you this, but your brother was D.O.A. We called you down here because we needed a relative to identify his body." Mylene watched as Reecee broke down. Reecee's body went numb as she looked at the man through her glassy eyes. "D.O.A? Identify his...NO!" She cried "NO!" God, NO!"

"I'm sorry for your loss," the doctor stated. His tone held no sympathy and he barely looked at Reecee as he delivered the worst news she ever received.

"I'll give you a few minutes, but I do still need you to ID the body," he walked out of the room without once looking back.

Reecee's screams could be heard through the entire emergency room. Tears fell from Mylene's eyes as she wrapped her arms around Trouble's sister. Reecee clung to Mylene and the two girls sat down, rocking each other back and forth in an attempt to deal with their grief.

Mylene looked toward the glass door at the sky as she held on to Reecee. Mylene let go when she saw the news flash across the waiting room TV. Nitro's picture was on the morning news. "Turn that up!" Mylene yelled as she jumped up, leaving Reecee's side and rushing to the nurse's station.

"Please turn that up!" She repeated. The nurse increased the volume on the TV and Mylene watched in desperation.

"Hi, this is Karen Johnson reporting live at Club Level in Tampa. Last night, this was the scene of a deadly shooting. Two people were shot and killed. These deaths bring the total to two hundred and thirty-seven in Tampa's murder count this year alone. Tampa it one of the most violent cities per Capita in America." Mylene shook her head in disbelief, hoping she was just dreaming. Mylene tuned the reporter out and rushed back to the Nurse's station.

"Can you please give me the room number for Michael Knight?" she asked with a puppy dog face. The nurse typed in Nitro's name and nodded her head.

"Mr. Knight is in room eight-fourteen." Mylene looked back toward Reecee, who was still grieving uncontrollably over the loss of her brother. She ran over to her and kneeled by her side.

"I'll be back, Reecee. I have to go check on Nitro." Mylene didn't believe the news that Nitro was one of the people that died. That's why when she asked the nurse what room he was in her heart felt at ease when the nurse gave her the answer she was looking for.

"Are you going to be okay? Mylene asked. Reecee nodded her head.

Mylene rushed to the nearest elevator in search of Nitro. She stepped inside and closed her eyes as she prepared herself for what she was about to see. Please, God, let him be okay.

Nitro was grateful that he was still alive, considered himself lucky to be breathing as he lay on the hospital bed. Something told him to put on his bullet proof vest before he stepped out that night and he was glad that he followed his instincts. His vest was the only thing that saved him from a certain death. One of the bullets had struck him in the shoulder, but most of them hit his vest, leaving him with some bad bruises and one gunshot wound. But he would rather have bruises and a bad shoulder than holes any day. Having seen Trouble get shot in the head, he couldn't help but feel that he had cheated death. The emotions that he felt for his best friend were overwhelming.

Trouble had been the only person who could call him brother. Even after the murder of his little brother Lil' Trill, Nitro really got closer to Trouble and his family. Trouble was like a real brother that he didn't have. Now Nitro had been forced to watch him die. The doctors had given him Vicodin to take some of his pain away and the potent prescription drug had him woozy. He could barely keep his eyes open, but he was paranoid that El Mayo wanted him dead, so he made an effort to stay awake. He also knew that the police would have some questions for him. They would want to know why he had acquired a bullet-proof vest, but he wasn't going to stick around and wait for them to question him. Nitro focused his attention on the door as Mylene walked into the room. The room was dark, but he still recognized her. He could tell by the way that she walked that it was her. Her steps were timid, and she was afraid of the condition that Nitro could be in.

"They got Trouble, Mylene. She blew his brains out right in front of me," he stated without looking up in her direction.

"Oh my God, thank you." She whispered as she walked to his bedside and kissed his cheek. Her mind wasn't on Trouble. She was just happy to see that Nitro hadn't joined him in death. She sobbed as she kissed his face over and over again. Tears from her eyes dripped onto his skin and he reached for her hand.

"Why are you crying, Ma?" he asked. "I don't know. I'm just glad you're okay. When you didn't come home like you told me, I thought..." She couldn't finish her sentence. "I'm right here, Mylene, I told you I'm not going anywhere. It's me and you against the world," he whispered as he graced her face with his fingertips.

"Yes!" She nodded her head with understanding. "Now help me out of this bed," he stated. "I got to get out of here before the Police come through." As Mylene helped him out of the bed he grimaced. She was careful not to touch his bandaged chest. "Are you sure you're okay to leave?" she asked. "Yeah, I'm good. I was wearing a vest, so the shots to the chest didn't penetrate. I took one in the shoulder though and my entire arm hurts like shit," he answered. Nitro reached for Mylene and she helped him stand, by putting one arm behind his back as he draped his good arm across her shoulder.

"Everything's gon' be alright, Mylene." "But what about you? You just got shot. Who did this to you?" Mylene stopped to look Nitro in the eyes. Nitro sighed as he felt the throbbing in his chest. "Your father put a hit on me." "Oh my God," she said with water forming up in her eyes like she was about to shed a tear. Nitro grabbed the back of Mylene's neck and brought her close as he kissed her on the lips.

"Do you trust me?" he asked. She nodded her head. "Let me hear you say it." "I trust you, Nitro." "All right then, like I told you before, you don't need to worry about anything." Mylene smiled slightly because she was finally where she wanted to be, right beside Nitro. Reminiscent of when the rapper Tupac Shakur had been ambushed and shot in New York City and then immediately checked himself out of the hospital against his doctors wishes. Nitro, fearing that his life was still in jeopardy, decided to pull a "Tupac Shakur," and checked himself out against medical advice.

Mylene held onto Nitro and helped him into a wheelchair and then wheeled him out of the hospital without ever looking back.

CHAPTER: 37 MY BROTHER'S KEEPER

REECEE STEPPED INTO THE COLD ROOM AND STARED at the bodies lying on the steel tables, covered with white sheets. Her heart felt as if it would explode from fear. Deep within, she knew that her brother was lying lifeless on one of these tables.

The coroner looked at the disheveled woman before him and pity filled her face. A police detective stood in the corner of the room and watched her every move as the coroner led her to one of the bodies. "Are you ready?" the woman asked as she put her hands on the white sheet. Reecee wanted to respond, but the huge lump in her throat stopped her from speaking.

After a couple of seconds, the Coroner pulled the covers back, revealing Trouble. Reecee's hand flew to her mouth as she doubled over in grief.

"Trouble! God, NO! NO!" she cried as she caressed her deceased brothers face. His skin was cold and held a blue hue. The one bullet hole that was in the center of his forehead had dried up blood crust around the wound. The Coroner nodded toward the Detective who then walked toward Reecee.

"Miss, when your brother was killed, he wasn't alone. We have another victim, a male, but we can't seem to find him. I think he checked himself out of the hospital before we could question him. Do you think you can give me that person's name? The one your brother was with at the time of the shooting?" the detective asked with his pen and pad out ready to write.

Reecee nodded her head and said "NO."

"How do you expect for me to help find your brother's killer and bring him to justice?"

"See that is the difference between me and you Cop. I don't need any help. I can do it on my own." Reecee said with a serious look before she walked off, leaving the detective with a Dumb founded look upon his face.

CHAPTER 38: YOU WILL PAY

NITRO & MYLENE PULLED UP TO HIS THREE-BEDROOM house and she helped him out of the cab and up the steps into the house. What they didn't know was that El Mayo already had his shooter sent out to the house. Nitro didn't let Mylene know it, but he was feeling a bit paranoid. He didn't want to take it this far with El Mayo, but now he left him with no choice. Killing his main man is like taking his last piece of heart that he had left. From losing all his loved ones throughout his life. He doesn't have any choice but to make El Mayo pay for taking his partner's life. Nitro really didn't want to go to his crib because he knew that by El Mayo talking with Angie, El Mayo knew where some of his spots were. Nitro wanted to avoid moving around too much, to make it seem like he was dead, just how the news pronounced it.

When they entered inside the house, Mylene helped him to the guestroom and sat him down on the edge of the bed. Nitro looked up at her and for the first time, he noticed Mylene was pouring down tears. He reached out for her hand and pulled her close to him.

"Why are you crying, Ma? He asked. "Because when you didn't come home, I got worried about you and called your phone. A female answered. I thought you were cheating on me." "What do you mean a female answered," "Yes, a female answered your phone and said that you were sleeping." Nitro had put two and two together and knew that was the same female that shot him and Trouble.

"Bae that was the same female that shot me and Trouble. Trouble met her in the Club that night." "Baby, what does she look like?" Mylene asked concerned. "She had light green eyes, dark brown skin, with jet black hair," Nitro said. "Oh my God baby, I know exactly who you're talking about. Kimbella!" Nitro looked Mylene in her eyes and asked, "Who is Kimbella?" "She is a professional killer my father hired a while back." Nitro knew that El Mayo sent the hit. Now it's time for him to take care of El Mayo like all the others he put six feet deep.

"Bae, go pack all your stuff, we're moving locations." he said as he stood up and walked over to grab his Glock 40 with the extended clip off the night stand.

"Baby what's wrong?" she asked. "Mylene, we don't have time for questions right now. Go get your stuff packed. Mylene did exactly what she was told. She left the bedroom to go pack her things. Nitro packed his bag with three automatic handguns but took one Glock 40 back out when he heard his dogs out back barking. Nitro knew the only time his dogs bark is when someone is close by. He cocked back the hammer on his gun then crept through the house, making his way toward the bedroom. Mylene had the bedroom door cracked. She didn't pay any attention to the masked gunman, creeping up on the side of the back porch. Nitro viewed the dark shadow and then bust inside the room, telling Mylene to get down. He let loose the whale clip, hitting his target through the glass window. Mylene let out a loud scream as she hit the floor, hearing nothing but gunfire ring out in the bedroom then glass shattering. Nitro ran on the side of the bed and grabbed Mylene by the arm and told her to stay behind him. Both ducked out the room and quickly made their way down the hallway. He stopped Mylene and told her to be quiet, because he didn't know how many people were inside the house. She nodded her head trying to stop the crying. Nitro threw down his Glock 40 when he realized the clip was empty.

"Damn," he said to himself. He left his guns behind, inside the bag. Mylene pulled out a 9mm from her waistline and handed it to Nitro. He cocked the hammer back, making sure there was a bullet inside the chamber. He saw another masked gunman creeping through the front door. He let off five shots, dropping the person at the door. Mylene covered her ears to block out the loud sound. Both exited the front door, jumped inside of a gray Range Rover and took off.

The next morning, Nitro awoke to excruciating pain shooting up and down the left side of his body. He knew that his arm would hurt but he had no idea how badly. He was careful not to disturb Mylene as he got out of the bed and made his way to the bathroom. He opened the medicine cabinet and retrieved some Tylenol. Taking three at a time, he hoped that the mild, over the counter drug, would relieve his pain. His thoughts drifted to Trouble and he gripped the sink in agony over the thought of losing his partner. Nitro made a promise to Trouble if anything ever happened to him, that he would take care of his kids. He looked in his bathroom mirror and saw Mylene enter the room. She walked up behind him and wrapped her arms around his body, resting her face on his toned upper back.

"Hey you," she greeted him with a sincere smile. "How do you feel?"

"I'm good," he replied as he turns around briefly to kiss her forehead.

"Just thinking about everything. I just can't believe I'm about to bury my man in a few days.

"Baby, I learned being in the game can get real deep, but you have to ask yourself, is all of this worth dying for? I understand that you lost your best friend, but understand me, I don't want to lose you," she said, as she kissed him on the back of his neck.

Nitro looked at his reflection in the mirror and thought to himself that it was too late to back out of the game now. After so many loved ones lost, he figured if he backs out now, that he is turning his back on the ones he lost in the game. Nitro felt that he had to keep GMC's name alive throughout the streets. Him and his partner put in work since day one and to just let it go like that. He knew that his time would come, but until then he was going to hold down them three letters until his casket drops.

CHAPTER 39: THE FUNERAL

Nitro sat in the limo along with Trouble's baby mother and son, while on their way to the funeral services. Tameka didn't go because she knew that the ceremony was under surveillance and she didn't want to put her job at risk by attending the services. Nitro supported Trouble's family during this devastating time. Sobs and lost hopes filled the air and it broke Nitro's heart to see Trouble's young son, smiling and playing, not grasping that his father was gone forever.

Nitro and Mylene sat front row with Trouble's family. They watched the Pastor preach over Trouble's white and gold trimmed casket. Reecee, Trouble's sister, kept whispering while quietly crying into a handkerchief, "He's gone, he's gone."

Nitro rested his hand on her shoulder and assured her that he would retaliate against the man that killed her brother. She kept asking Nitro what went on that night and he told her everything, not leaving out anything.

"Everything is going to be alright," Nitro said confidently as Reecee shed tears. Nitro held her gently in his arms. Nitro noticed

Mylene was rubbing Trouble's mothers back, keeping her at ease. Trouble's baby mother, Stacy, had her son in her arms rocking him back and forth. With her tears, she soaked his father's memorial shirt that he was wearing. Nitro knew that Trouble's funeral was littered with undercover cops who likely wanted to question him, but he didn't care at that point. Everything was about Trouble. With the way he was feeling, he knew that he would probably go to jail for murdering a cop with his bare hands, if they were to be disrespectful and approach him at the funeral.

The walk to Trouble's casket seemed like it was three miles long to Nitro. He looked down at Trouble's body and was at a loss for thoughts and words. Seeing a man that was so close to him lying in a casket taught him a lesson, nobody was untouchable.

After the service, Nitro sat with the family at Trouble's mother's estate, just outside of Clearwater, in the Suburb of Black Dr. Nitro never knew that Trouble bought his mother a house. He thought she was still staying in Largo, but never knew that he moved his mother close by.

Trouble was a certified gangsta from the projects and he knew a gangsta in the game was either murdered or locked up. Nitro was quiet as he stared out of the living room window, thinking about the times he and Trouble had. His mind was so far gone, and he couldn't stop the play button from going off in his head, telling him retaliation is a must. All of Trouble's family members were scattered around the room, grieving in sorrow. Nitro felt someone gently pat him on his right leg and he turned to see Trouble's son Lil' Terry standing before him, with a fresh Mohawk haircut.

"What's up Uncle Nitro?" Lil' Terry said with his toy airplane in his hand. Nitro kneeled down to get to Lil' Terry's height.

"Hey Lil' man. How you doing?" he asked, bringing Lil' Terry close into his arms, giving him a hug.

"I am doing good Uncle. Did you see my daddy sleeping in that box? My mama said that it's not a box, it is a casket. Can you tell me what it is Uncle Nitro? Because sometimes my mama doesn't know what she is talking about." Nitro let out a little laugh and then answered Trouble's son's question. "Your mother is right Lil' man, your father is resting in a casket." Nitro replied back looking Lil' Terry into his dark brown eyes.

"When is he going to get up?" Lil' Terry asked, taking a hold of Nitro's diamond chain that was around his neck. Nitro took a deep breath in before he answered Trouble's son's question,

"Listen to me Lil' man, your father is up in heaven with your Uncle Trill, both of them are together in a better place," Nitro said emotionally.

"My mama said that my daddy got his angel wings and he flew deep up into the sky like an airplane," he said flying his toy plane around in the air.

"He sure did Lil' man." Nitro said trying to hold back his tears.

"Well, is he coming back to get me?" Lil' Terry asked as he watched Nitro shed a tear. It was hard for Nitro to answer that question, because he knew that his father wasn't coming back but he had to tell him the truth.

"Lil' man, your father is not coming back, but always remember this, he is going to be with you every step you take in life", Nitro said as he patted him on the shoulder. "You're the man of the house now, so you have to protect your mother," Nitro said with tears snaking down his face. Nitro hugged Trouble's son tightly in his arms. Trouble's mother Ms. Roof walked up wearing a black and white Dior dress.

"Lil' Terry, your mother is looking for you" she said to her grandson. Nitro let go of him and he took off running out back.

"Chiiiiild! What am I going to do with him? He looks just like his father," Ms. Roof said with her two solid gold teeth shining at the top of her mouth. Ms. Roof sat back and watched her grandson run out the back door.

"How are my other sons holding up?" Ms. Roof asked Nitro as she gave him a hug and kiss on his cheek.

"I am hanging in there Ms. Roof. I just can't believe he's gone." he replied back.

"He was just talking about you before he left the house that night. Telling me how he was going to surprise you by letting you know that he has a baby on the way. He promised me that once the baby was delivered into this world, he was going to leave them streets alone."

Ms. Roof said, taking her white handkerchief out of her top pocket and wiping her tears away from her eyes.

"Now I only have two sons left, you and Israel. I Pray that you both please get out them streets. Those streets are not a good place to be. A bullet does not have a name on it and these young people out here are just killing for no reason, just because someone looked at you wrong!" Nitro nodded his head agreeing with Ms. Roof and everything she was saying. Nitro dropped his head, as a wave of guilt overcame him. Ms. Roof gently lifted his head with her index finger and stared him in the eyes.

"It's not your fault," she said.

"Trouble was his own man and made his own decisions. That boy ran the streets at the age of ten. He was so deep into the streets I knew that it would be hard to pull him out. Ever since I moved into Jordan Park and he started to hang with them project kids, I knew that he was going to be a problem," she said as she wiped away the tears that were racing down her face. Nitro took Ms. Roof into his arms and told her that everything was going to be alright.

CHAPTER 40: I'M BACK!

AFTER A COUPLE OF SHOOTOUTS AND DEAD BODIES dropping down left and right, Nitro and GMC was still at war with El Mayo and Ghost. Three weeks after Trouble's funeral, Nitro turned up in the streets shooting everything and everyone connected to Ghost and his crew.

Ghost had got word from one of his henchmen that Nitro wasn't dead. Ghost immediately notified El Mayo, letting him know that Nitro was still alive. Nitro was on his way to meet wth one of his Lil' Niggas that hung out in Bethel Heights projects when he got word that Ghost had something to do with him getting shot. Word had got out that Ghost was in the Club at the time of the shooting. Nitro whipped his black-on-black Chevy Suburban inside of the broke down housing complex. The building looked like it had to be painted over several times, to where the owner just gave up hope. The one way in and one way out complex looked like a desert storm.

Clothes were hanging from several windows, along with cable lines running from window to window. Bebe kids were running around throughout the complex with toy water guns. You had a couple of ratchet females standing out in the crowded parking lot gossiping amongst each other, talking about who fucked who's baby father. Nitro spotted C-Dub standing on the sidewalk talking to a thick red boned chic. C- Dub quickly stopped the conversation when he noticed a black Suburban parked right across from him, flashing its lights. C-Dub told the girl to excuse him for a minute while he goes to check and see who was inside the Suburban. C-Dub called Nitro and told him to stop by, so he could give him the latest news on his enemy Ghost, so C-Dub had an idea of who was in the Suburban. C-Dub walked up to the front of the dark tinted Suburban and ducked down a little, so he could get a good view inside the truck. He saw a hand wave at him through the glass telling him to get inside. C-Dub moved quickly when he caught view of Nitro's face. C-Dub headed toward the passenger's side door and jumped inside.

"Damn Nigga, what you thought I was them people or something," Nitro said wearing a black skull cap with an all-black hoodie sweatshirt.

"Hell yeah, Nigga. You told me that you were on your way, but you didn't tell me what you were riding in." C-Dub replied, giving Nitro some dap with a grin on his face.

"My bad Lil' bra, I forgot to tell you that. So, what is the word?" Nitro asked.

"Okay check it, this Nigga is going to be at Club Dollar tonight. A new strip joint they just opened, right across from the Seven-Eleven. I already set up everything. Our girl Nicki is going to do the honors," C-Dub said pointing his finger at Nicki, who was still standing by rolling up a blunt. Nitro turned his head towards Nicki and then said,

"Dammm, that's Nicki? She done got thicker than a mutha fucker."

"Hell yeah, that's that Baby. She got shot, went to prison, did a little bid and got out looking stupid thick," C-Dub said.

"Yes, lord she is," Nitro said thinking about telling Nicki to jump inside taking her for a ride, but he knew that he had something even thicker waiting at the house for him.

"So, everything is already set up?" Nitro asked.

"Everything is a green light. Nicki met that pussy three nights ago and he fell for her beauty." C-Dub replied. Nitro grinned because he knew that he had Ghost right where he wants him, six feet deep in the dirt.

Nitro reached behind him grabbing a black bookbag that had twenty bands inside. He threw the bag on C-Dub's lap and said, "Everything is there. Make sure that everything goes as planned." C-Dub grabbed the bag, unzipped it, then opened it up. His eyes got big when he saw the piles of one-hundred-dollar bills wrapped up in rubber bands.

"Listen Fam, you got my word everything will go right. I just need you to be present, only to put a little bit of icing on the cake," C-Dub said as he gave Nitro some dap, before exiting the truck. Nitro pulled out of the parking lot ready for the set-up.

Minutes later, Nitro pulled up at Tameka's house. After Trouble's death, he had been stopping by more often to see how she was holding up. He got out of the car and walked up to her front steps to knock on the door. Tameka on the other end of the door was fixing herself a glass of orange juice, when she heard three knocks at her door. She put her glass down, to see who could be knocking at her door. She walked vastly to the door and looked through the peep hole. She saw Nitro standing on her front porch holding a set of red roses and balloons. She unlocked her door and opened it for him to come in. Nitro greeted her with a smile and a kiss on her cheek as he stepped off inside the house.

"Heyyy, Nitro!! How you been doing?" she asked, as he handed her the roses and balloons.

"I am doing alright and yourself?"

"I am trying to make it through. This girl of mine just won't stop kicking," Tameka said as she walked over to her living room table sitting down the roses and balloons.

"Thank you for the gift," Tameka said with a smile.

"No problem. I was already over this way, so I wanted to stop by and check up on you," Nitro replied.

"Look at you, that stomach is getting big as a house." Nitro joked.

"I know, it's like she's growing every minute," Tameka said with a grin, as she rubbed her basketball stomach through her yellow and green sundress.

"Please have a seat, make yourself at home. Would you like anything to drink?" Tameka asked, walking back towards the kitchen.

"No, thank you, I'm alright," Nitro replied as he sat down on Tameka's soft leather couch, taking in the décor. He can tell that she changed around a couple of things since the last time he stopped by. Nitro took sight of a picture with Trouble hugging Tameka from behind. He grabbed a hold of the picture off the table and then rested his hand across the picture, mourning the loss of his partner.

"We took that picture on my birthday. Three days before his death," Tameka said walking out of the kitchen with a glass of orange juice in her hand, taking a seat right next to him. Nitro inhaled a deep breath before letting loose.

"I just wish he was here to see his daughter born," He said emotionally.

"I never asked what happened that night because I figured that it was too early, and a lot was going on. Nitro, please tell me what happened that night?"

Nitro put down the picture he was holding and then turned towards Tameka to tell her what happened. It's like he told the story a million times over and over, but he only told it once and that was to Trouble's sister Reecee. After twenty minutes of talking, Nitro told Tameka everything.

"Nitro, El Mayo is a really dangerous man. I didn't know ya'll was in business. The Feds had El Mayo under investigation many times but couldn't nail him. You be careful because a couple of weeks ago, they found a body of a girl named Angie Brown laying in her home, dead, with gunshot wounds. Feds believe that it was one of El Mayo's girls because they found several picture's inside the house."

Nitro sat and listened as Tameka continued, not knowing that he was the one who killed Angie. Tameka probably wouldn't care if Nitro told her that he was the one who took Angie's life. She was already down with the team. Nitro remembered when Trouble was telling him that Tameka said Pacman needed to die because he was a snitch. He liked that Tameka was down for the cause, but some things just can't be discussed. Tameka was still a cop.

After wrapping up the conversation, Nitro was on his way home. He pulled up in the driveway of his home. Mylene walked over to the living room window with an AR-15 assault rifle in her hand after she heard a car door slam. Mylene peeked out the window and noticed

Nitro carrying a KFC bag. That quickly put a smile on her face. She rushed to the front door to let Nitro in.

"Hey baby," Mylene said as she opened the door. Nitro viewed the powerful weapon she had in her hand before he spoke.

"Everything alright?" Nitro asked as he gives her a kiss on the lips.

"Yes, everything is alright. Your father called the house looking for you. He said that he couldn't reach you on your phone. I told him as soon as you walk in, I will tell you to call him," Mylene said as she laid the AR-15 on the couch.

"Oh yeah! I haven't gotten a call from him in a couple of days," Nitro replied as he sat the KFC bag down on the kitchen table and then pulled his cellphone out of his front pocket. He recognizes that his phone was dead. Nitro took his phone and plugged it into the phone charger that was in the kitchen.

"Bae, I stopped by and grabbed you something to eat. I figured that you were hungry."

"Thank you, baby. You read my mind. I do have a taste for some chicken, but first I would like to have that steak bone inside those jeans," Mylene said as she walked up on Nitro, forcing her tongue down his throat. Mylene unfastened his belt buckle letting his pants fall to his ankles. She pulled his Polo boxers halfway down to his knees, before she took a hold of his pole, putting it inside her mouth. Nitro's eyes rolled to the back of his head when he felt the warmness of her mouth. She moaned as she stroked him back and forth with him still inside her mouth. Nitro gripped the counter as she picks up her pace, he was in the zone. Her every moan only made him harder. He stood Mylene up on her feet and then whispered, "Daddy's turn," he lifted her black Prada dress and picked her up. He placed her on the kitchen counter, pulled her panties to the side and fell deep inside of her fat, wet, pussy. Within minutes, he was on the verge of busting a nut.

"Nitro, be gentle," she pleaded just as he was on the edge. Ignoring her call for mercy, he continued to slide in her wetness, not missing a wall on the way in or out.

"Shit!" he said as he began to bust long and hard. As the last drop drained from his body, he pushed all the way in. Mylene inhaled as he ran his soft tongue along her neck and back.

"Damn, baby. The pussy is hot. I'll need some more of that," he whispered in her ear as he pulls out. Taking his dick in his hand, he began stroking himself back to full potential.

"Baby, wait!" she said. Ignoring her pleas again, Nitro kissed her hungrily, he figured she wanted the T-bone steak and she get what she asked for.

"Baby," she called out. But Nitro was focused as if she hadn't said a word.

"Nitrooo," she moaned, as he began to lick on her breasts. Placing his mouth over her nipple, he sucked gently as he slid in fast and hard. Nitro sucked and licked harder on her nipple as he hit the bottom with very forceful blows. Moving back, Mylene tried to escape all those inches.

"Come here," he growled, pulling her back to the edge of the counter. Sensing her struggle, he grabbed her legs and threw them over his shoulders. Holding her in place, he went to work, again finding it hard to hold back. The pussy was wetter and hotter than usual.

"This is what you want huh," Nitro said as he nailed inside her with force.

After about twenty more minutes, he was again on edge.

"Ssss ... baby, baby, baby," he moaned as he again released his passion all the way inside her. Mylene arched her back and received all of him out of breath and satisfied, Nitro pulled her to him. Kissing and sucking her lips, he looked in her eyes.

"What did you do to my pussy while I was gone?" he asked, as he held her tenderly in his arms. Mylene grabbed him around his neck and whispered in his ear, "I'm pregnant."

Nitro awoke at 10:00PM. He spent hours holding Mylene and rubbing her belly, excited that she was pregnant. She could not stop him from smiling.

"Oh shit!" Nitro said as he looked at the clock on the night stand.

"What's up baby? What's wrong?" Mylene asked as she watched Nitro jump out of bed and start to put on clothes.

"I got this set-up going down and I have to be there. I got the drop on that nigga Ghost who I was telling you about," Nitro said as he grabbed his black hoodie sweater out of the closet.

"Baby let me go with you," she asked with a pleading look.

"No Mylene. Shit might get ugly and I don't need you around any danger," he replied as he threw on the sweater over his white tee.

"I don't need you anywhere around when this shit pop off." Mylene leaned her head back against the headboard with her arms crossed over her breasts, face balled up, mad that she can't go to back up her man.

"I thought we were in this together," she said, looking at Nitro grabbing a 9mm, screw on silencer, out of the top dresser drawer.

"Baby, we're in this together, but I don't need you out and about right now. I need you to take care of that baby girl that's in your stomach right there," he said with a grin.

"How do you know it's a girl?" Mylene asked with a smile.

"Because I already have a boy," he replied, as he kissed Mylene on her lips.

"You be careful," she said, hoping Nitro would change his mind and tell her to put on some clothes.

"I will, Bae," he replied before walking out the bedroom door. He stopped by the kitchen to grab his cellphone off the charger.

Mylene stood at the living room window with the AR-15 in her hand as she watched Nitro get inside the car. She shook her head before saying a silent prayer.

CHAPTER 41: THE POP OFF

NITRO PULLED UP IN FRONT OF CLUB DOLLAR, CHECKING out the scene before he parked on the side of the building. He reached inside of his black bag and pulled out a small walkie-talkie. He radioed into the ones he had positioned, making sure that everyone was on point. Nitro had radioed in to Gunz who was inside the club, keeping eyes on Ghost. The Pirate Kids were positioned out front of the club in an all-white stolen van. Just in case Ghost escapes the hit, they'll pick up the Slack.

"Everything is a 10-4," Gunz radioed back. Nitro stuffed the walkie-talkie in his front pocket and pulled out his 9mm from his bag. He checked the clip, making sure he has enough ammo inside. He cocked back the hammer on the gun, putting one inside the chamber before he exited the vehicle, making his way inside the club.

Club Dollar was packed, working with a full house tonight. Nitro made his way through the jam-packed club. He had his black hoodie real low as he mobbed through a large crowd.

Nicki was on stage working the pole as she looked out into the crowd. She noticed the club was jam-packed like always when she worked. Dollar bills were scattered all over the stage during her show. Nicki didn't dance at the club on a regular, so it was always a treat for the regular patrons when she did. She was always sure to call her regular customers and let them know when she was going to be taking the stage. She knew that they would be there to spread the love in the form of dollar bills and buy some expensive drinks. She was known to have dudes buy her hundred-dollar drinks. As Keith Sweat's Song, "Chocolate Girl" played Nicki put on the show of her life. Sliding down the pole upside down spread eagle. She slowly straightened her legs and kicked them down, rising into a standing position as she looked out at the clapping crowd of men who had enjoyed her little stunt. She watched as they marched up to the stage like an army of ants, but instead of carrying breadcrumbs they had them bands. She even allowed a couple to stick some down her Camisole, allowing them to get a quick free feel of her breasts. A satisfying smile spread across face's as she looked out. Nicki reached high on the pole and gripped it hard with her thighs. This allowed her body to hang upside down once again. She then slowly slid down. This time her little trick caught Ghost's attention. She winked at him as she made her way down to the button of the pole. She then put her shaved bald pussy in a customer's face and did a slow grind. The man stuck out his tongue and licked her slowly. He had full access to her because of the crotchless camisole she was wearing. The crowd went crazy when they saw the man feasting on her. Nicki wasn't embarrassed or ashamed by the performance. She was all about her paper and was willing to do whatever it took to get it. She had made a name for herself as one of the best dancers in St. Pete. She had the body of a goddess. The kind of body a man would crave for. Nitro sat in a dark corner with dim lights as he watched her walk over to Ghost's table, taking a seat in his lap.

"Damn ma, you just going to let that old fuck lick my pussy like that?" Ghost asked.

"Ghost, why you tripping? He is a paying customer and besides, he only licked the pussy for a minute," she replied back.

"Shiiit, that was long enough. How long can I lick the pussy for the night? Ghost asked.

"For as long as you want to baby." she said kissing him on the side of his neck, catching sight of Nitro sitting in the corner. She then winked her eye at him letting him know that she is working her magic. Ghost had four of his goons sitting around him at the table, plus a big black heavy-set security guard.

Somehow Nicki got Ghost to leave without his goons following behind. Nitro peeped the play and bee lined right behind them. Making it upstairs into the dimly lit hallway. Nitro saw Ghost handing a muscle-bound security guard some money to stand and guard the door while he goes and plays.

"Damn baby, Can I take you home with me for the night? The drunk white girl asked, pushing herself up against Nitro. Nitro looked at the white girl and grinned as he held her in his arms. Nitro didn't know what to say. He looked around hoping the drunk girl don't blow his cover.

"I don't have on no panties," she whispered in his ear, taking his hand and sliding it under her dress. He felt how wet the girl was and his dick went from soft to hard. He was hoping that someone was with the girl, but he didn't see anyone around. The security guard started to take notice down the hall.

"Bunny, what the hell are you doing down this hallway?" Another blonde asked.

"Thank you, Lord," Nitro said to himself.

"Excuse me, but this is my friend," the white girl said. Nitro threw up his hands and said,

"Feel free."

"Thank you," the girl said as she drags her friend by the arm.

Nitro reached under his shirt and pulled out a 9mm from his waistline, putting it inside his front sweater pockets. He walks up to the security guard and gets stopped at the door.

"Yo, you can't come in here, the room is already taken," he said, stopping Nitro with his hands from coming in.

"It's not nice to put your hands on a boss," he said before pulling out his gun and letting off two shots into the guard's stomach.

Nitro eased the man's body down slowly, stopping him from hitting the floor hard. He steps inside the room where he notices Ghost laid up next to Nicki in the bed.

"Ghost what's up?" Nitro said putting flame to a blunt.

Ghost's eyes got wide. He was surprised to see Nitro standing right in front of him. Nicki had pulled out a 3-80 from underneath the pillows.

"What the —," Ghost didn't get a chance to finish his sentence before brains and tissue blew out of the side of his head. She watched his body fall to the side and then slid out of bed, grabbing all her belongings in her hand. She walked up to Nitro, giving him a kiss on the side of his cheek like a real boss.

"Job is done," she said in a sexy tone of voice. Nitro watched her ass jiggle walking out of the door. He grinned as he viewed Ghost's body slumped over the bed.

"Check mate, bitch ass Nigga," Nitro said before he turned around to walk out the door.

Nitro was on his way back home, he felt bad for taking Angie's life in the house. He just got word from Nicki that Angie wasn't the one that told EI Mayo, it was Ghost. Ghost had told Nicki everything he had going on in the streets. He was a sucker for love. Nicki also knew about two stash houses Ghost has. She wasn't going to tell Nitro, because she figured that she was paid for the set-up, not to give out information. The two stash spots were her come up and no one else knew about them.

It was still night out and Nicki pulled up at a blue and white house, with a brown wooden gate around it. She noticed Greedy's smoke gray BMW sitting out front.

"What the fuck is he doing here?" she said to herself.

Nicki took a minute to think to herself if she still wanted to pull off the lick. She didn't know if Greedy got word yet about Ghost being dead.

"Fuck it, let's go," She said to herself as motivation, before grabbing her all-black Chanel handbag, getting out of her Volvo S60 and walking up to the door.

She knocked twice on the door before Greedy opened it. "What's up Greedy?" she said with a fake smile.

"What's up with you," Greedy replied, as he looked at Nicki wearing a short blue tight dress that stopped at her knees.

"Ghost told me to stop by and wait for him after I got done dancing at the Club." Nicki threw a small lie at Greedy just for him to let her inside. Greedy didn't have a problem letting her in.

"Come in, lock the door behind you," he said, walking back over to take a seat on the couch.

Nicki stepped inside and did exactly what she was told and locked the door. Then she took a seat.

"Nicki what's up? I thought you was going to put me down with your girlfriend," Greedy said taking the blunt from behind his ear.

"I told her you said that you wanted to get with her. She said that she was going to let me know something after she comes back from Atlanta," Nicki said with her legs crossed. She knew that she didn't have much time, before someone called his phone. Greedy didn't get a chance to say another word, before she quickly drew out her Chrome 38 and pointed it directly at his face.

"Nicki what's up?" Greedy said as he stared inside the barrel of Nicki's gun.

"Nigga, don't what's up me. You thought I was young, dumb and full of cum! Now It's time to play hard ball Nigga! You're going to open the safe in the bathroom, where Ghost got all the Cash and dope."

"Pow!" Nicki shot him in the thigh.

"That's just to let you know I'm not fucking around with you Nigga! Tell me what the fuck I want to know, or I'll shoot your dick off next!"

"Okay, Okay, don't shoot," Greedy cried out, holding one hand up in the air and the other one on his gunshot wound.

"Pussy nigga, get to hopping like a frog, before I let off another shot in this mutha fucka." She watched as he hopped his way towards the bathroom. Greedy tried to hold himself up as he took down a picture on the wall that covered the safe.

"Hurry nigga," she said with her gun pointed to the back of his head. He quickly punched in the numbers to the safe and opened it. Nicki had a grin on her face when she saw a safe full of cash, stacked up neatly. She didn't waste any time blowing Greedy's brains out all over the wall. Some blood even got on the money, but she didn't care as long as she got what she had come for. She watched as Greedy's body hit the floor. Blood seeped from his forehead onto the bathroom tiles. She rushed out of the bathroom into the bedroom to snatch a pillowcase off the bed. She went back into the bathroom and cleaned out the safe before fleeing the scene.

Nicki was on her way to hit her next target when she felt her phone vibrate in her lap.

Bzzzzzzzzz… Bzzzzzzzzz… Bzzzzzzzzz

She grabbed her phone and read a text from C-Dub.

"Are you alright?"

She quickly text back.

"Yes."

Nitro stepped inside the house with his gun drawn. He noticed all the lights off inside the house. He eased the door closed behind him, before creeping through. Nitro approached the bedroom door where the lights were on. He pushed the door open a little and witnessed Mylene in bed with the AR-15 next to her, she was snoring like a baby. Nitro grinned before stripping down to his boxers. He climbed into bed next to her, putting one arm around her as she opened her eyes.

"Hey Baby, did everything go right?" She whispered.

"Yes Bae, everything went just fine. That pussy is laying in a puddle of his own blood. Now the only one we have left is your farther and I am going to need your help with him," he said, thinking that he can use Mylene to get El Mayo right where he needed him.

"I don't have any problem with that. Just let me know when it's time," Mylene replied.

The following morning C-Dub stepped inside Nicki's apartment unexpectedly. He tried calling her but didn't get an answer. He thought something was wrong, so he stopped by to check on her. Nicki was in her bedroom doing the money dance. She didn't hear a sound as C-Dub stepped through her front door. She was too busy cheering herself on, looking at all the money and dope she had spread out on the bed.

C-Dub busted inside the room with his gun in hand after hearing noises coming from the room. Nicki quickly grabbed her 38 off the bed.

"Nicki, what the fuck—," C-Dub couldn't finish his sentence when he laid eyes on all the money and dope that was spread out on her bed.

Nicki was shocked to see C-Dub got inside her house. She thought that she locked the door. C-Dub balled his face up making an evil expression, thinking Nicki had held back information about Ghost. Both didn't say a word, before firing their guns at each other.

C-Dub hit the floor the same time as Nicki. C-Dub caught a gunshot wound to the right side of his lungs. Nicki suffered a gunshot wound to her intestine. She was on her last breath before kicking the bucket. C-Dub already went to meet his maker. Both laid in a small pool of blood.

"Nicki, is everything alright?" Sonya bawled out as she walked through Nicki's front door. She had heard some loud noises that sound like gunshots, so she made it her business to stop what she was doing and walk over to check on her friend. Once Sonya made it to the bedroom, she peeked her head inside and seen C-Dub and Nicki stretched out on the floor in a puddle of blood.

"Oh my God," she said with her hands covering her mouth.

Sonya stepped over C-Dub's body and rushed over to see about her friend. She could see there wasn't any hope for Nicki, she was already dead with blood running down the side of her mouth.

Sonya took notice of the money and dope that was laid out on the bed. She asked herself "What Could have gone wrong?" Sonya knew that she didn't have time to stand around, before the police come. She took the empty pillowcase that was next to the money and started to fill the bag. Sonya had got everything inside the pillowcase then left the scene.

CHAPTER 42: QUITTING THE GAME

IT'S BEEN SEVEN AND A HALF MONTHS AND MYLENE'S stomach was the size of a balloon. Nitro's beef was still heavy in the streets. He tried using Mylene to get close to El Mayo, but it didn't work. El Mayo already made up his mind and said that he is going to kill the both of them.

"Bae, I made you some coffee." Nitro shouted out from the kitchen. Mylene was sitting on the couch with her phone in her lap. Nitro walked out of the kitchen with two cups in his hands.

"Bae, what's wrong? Why do you have a sad expression on your face?" he asked as he handed her the coffee.

"Nitro, what are we going to do?" he is not answering the phone for me."

"Listen Bae, don't worry about your father. I told you that I will handle that, I just have to come up with plan b."

"Babe, why can't we just move? We have a family now and my father will not stop coming for us, unless we are dead," she said, looking Nitro in his eyes. Nitro felt if he left, then he would be letting Trouble and the rest of his loved ones that he lost in the Game down.

"I can't leave right now. GMC needs me."

"Nitro, I need you," She cries out, putting down her coffee on the table.

"Mylene, what do you want me to do?"

"I want you to use your head, we have a baby on the way." She replied.

"I understand that Bae, but I am not going to let anyone run me from my city."

"Nitro, it's not about anyone running you out of the city. It's about the family you have to look out for. My father sees things different. All my life I was raised with money. My father spoiled me. I was his little girl. I couldn't date guys when I got older. All I am trying to say is, Bae, I don't want our daughter to grow up how I did. I want you to leave the game alone. We have enough money why can't we just leave all this stuff behind? I need you and your children need you here the most. I know about your past and you losing your unborn child. I know you were in a lot of pain, but know this, I am here for you," Mylene said with her hand on his shoulder. Mylene got up and kissed Nitro on the lips before she walked in the kitchen. Nitro had sat and thought hard about what Mylene was saying. He thinks he should give the game a break...

Mylene touched a spot in his heart he thought no one would after Brenda passed. Deep down inside his heart, he really wanted to live a normal life, without looking over his shoulder. His heart was still with Brenda and his unborn child that he lost, and nothing would change that, but now he had to think about the future.

"Babe, I grabbed your phone out the room. Your father is on the line," she said as she walked out the bedroom with her purse strapped over her shoulder, giving him the phone.

"Pop's what's up? I will be through there in two hours. Me and Mylene are on our way to Chili's to sit down and eat. I will grab you a doggy bag," he said with a laugh before hanging up.

Nitro and Mylene jumped into the car and rode twelve blocks from the house, before stopping at a red light. An unknown person pulled up on the passenger side of Mylene, riding on A Ninja Bike and opened fire with a Cobray M-11.

"Oh shit! Get down, get down," Nitro cried out as he reached for his gun that was between the seat and safety box.

TAT, TAT, TAT, TAT, TAT, TAT

He couldn't get a hold of his gun, because it had slid down to the back floor of the car. Nitro put his special-edition 2015 Ford Mustang to the floor, catching out through traffic, getting away from the gun fire. Nitro kept reaching for his hammer as he drove, until he was finally able to grab it. Once he felt the cold steel in his hands, he was about to shoot back, but as he lifted the gun, he glanced over and saw Mylene on the passenger side of the car, with blood gushing out of her wounds. He froze, slamming on the brakes as he bent the corner, causing the Ninja Bike to miss the turn. He headed straight for the hospital. He knew there was no time to call an ambulance.

"Baby, just hold on."

"Okay, Nitro." she nodded.

"I love you!"

"I know," he said, tears rolling down his face along with the balls of perspiration.

"I love you, Baby!" Take care of the baby and remember I love you," she said in between breaths. She wanted Nitro to know that it didn't matter what her destiny was, if she lived or if she died. It was forever for them. She would always be in his heart and he was everything that she needed and longed for. "Until ..."

"Baby don't talk." He interrupted her as he rubbed her hand and tried to keep his eyes on the road. He didn't want to hear those words from Mylene. Until death do us part, because those words, the same words Brenda had uttered to him before she took her last breath, seemed to be a curse to him. Nitro knew there wasn't much time. She had been hit by bullets. They were no 22 bullets; they were assassin's bullets.

"Hold on, baby, please. Please hold on. I'm begging you" Nitro pleaded as tears ran down his face.

Nitro pulled up to the emergency room, screaming for the doctors. Two attendants rushed out and took Mylene away. While the doctors fought for Mylene's life, Nitro paced the hallway. It had only been a few hours since the doctor informed Nitro it would be at least twelve hours before Mylene was out of surgery. He never did promise that she would come out of it alive. Since then, Nitro tried getting into the operating room three times. He needed to see her. He was fully aware that this might be his last chance to see the love of his life alive. He needed and wanted to be by Mylene's side. On the third attempt a security Guard told him if he didn't calm down, the hospital would be forced to call the police and have him removed. Nitro really didn't give a fuck if they called the fucking National Guard, but he didn't want to distract the doctors from doing their jobs. Saving Mylene's life and his child's life as well. He needed some fresh air so that he would be able to think straight. He knew he had to regain his composure if he was going be any help to Mylene. Before leaving, Nitro gave the guard a mean look. He knew the toy cop was just doing his job, but Nitro also knew that if he ever ran into the rent-cop outside of the hospital it would take more will power than he possessed to keep from tearing into his ass.

The guard would have to pay for keeping him away from Mylene and his unborn child. It might cost him a little, it might cost him a lot, but it was going to cost him, and he was going to pay every dime.

Mylene's friend Hailie came to the hospital to sit with Nitro when she got a call, letting her know that Mylene had been shot.

The doctors walked out the door, Nitro and Hailie rushed up to the two doctors to see what they had to say. Judging by all Mylene's blood on their smocks the doctors looked like they had been operating on soldiers in Iraq instead of Mylene.

"We've done all we can do," one doctor said, and Hailie screamed at the top of her lungs, "Noooo!" The doctor put his hand up to try to get Hailie to calm down and listen "Nooo!!! Lord, don't do this to me." Hailie continued. Nitro put his arm around Hailie because he didn't believe what the doctor was about to say.

"Let him finish," Nitro said in a comforting way and looked at the doctor as he continued. "As I said, we've done all we can do at this time. At this point it's all up to Mylene. The Next hours to come are vital. If she can make it through the next seventy-two hours, then she and the baby should be all right. We were not comfortable giving an emergency C-Section, but the baby is fine. As I said, if she can fight and pull through the next seventy-two hours, she should be able to make a full recovery. At this point it's up to her. How hard she fights and how badly she wants to live."

"There's gotta be something else you can do." Nitro said. "Honestly, Sir, it's out of our hands. We've done everything we can."

Nitro spoke up, "Look, money isn't an issue. We are not poor black people with no insurance."

"Money won't make a difference," the doctor said.

"Can't we fly some more doctors in and do something? More experienced?" The doctor looked at Nitro and said with a bit of cockiness, "We are the best. In the late eighties, early nineties, St. Pete was the murder capital, and we saw countless gunshot victims and pulled them through. So, we are the best at what we do, but as good as we are, unfortunately it's out of our hands." The doctor looked at the family as if he wished there were more he could say, but there wasn't. Nitro muttered, "It's got to be something else we can do." The doctor looked him with a solemn face and said, "All any of us can do at this point is pray." Nitro sat by Mylene's bedside. as her heart monitor line crawled across the screen and beeped slowly. He took heed to what the doctor said and prayed like never before.

"God, I know I never really asked you for anything or been big into the whole religion thing. God, I am asking you, I am begging you to spare Mylene's and my baby's life. God, you know like I know that I turned into a cold nigga with an iron heart. Never did I think it was possible for me to love again and especially after I lost Brenda, my first love. So, I know the only way I could ever end up loving again, like I love Mylene, was your will. Thank you for bringing someone back into my life. I know God gives and takes, but please don't take her from me. I know I have to be accountable for all the lives I've taken away. I ask you for forgiveness of my sins and please don't take my family away. God, you know my heart.

Never in his life had Nitro called upon God like this. As he studied the green line on the life-support machine, he finally surrendered his own will and gave in to the will of God.

Tears came to his eyes as he talked to Mylene. "Baby, I always wondered what you ever wanted with a Nigga like me. I always felt like you deserved so much more, but you always said that I was all you needed. Well, I need you, baby. I know you know that I'm nothing without you. After my first love, I wasn't complete until you came into my life. Not only do I need you, I need you to be strong for our baby." He poured his heart out to her.

"This is the baby that you wanted. Remember in Miami, you made me promise that I will never leave you. Well, please don't leave me. I love you, baby. Please don't make our life in vain. You have made an important impact on my life," he tried to wipe his tears away, but he couldn't stop them from coming. He began to sob and when he did, he heard the beeps go quicker and the lines begin to go higher. Was that a sign that God heard his prayers and Mylene could hear every word he was saying. A sign that she was going to fight like hell to make it through?

Be tuned in. GMC Book 3 coming soon.

James Allen Neal (Sep. 12, 1951 - Jun 22, 2010),
Annie Doris Neal (Apr 18, 1958 - Dec 30, 2012)

**In loving memory of
James Allen Neal, Annie Doris Neal
Rest in heaven**

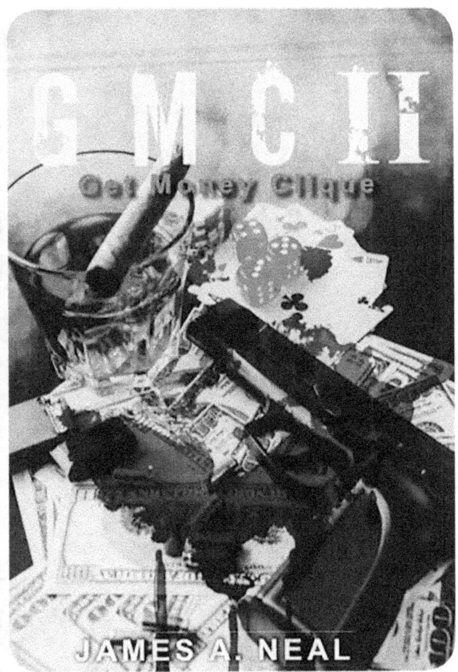

Reach me at this address:

Street Dreams LLC
PO BOX 531061
St. Petersburg, FL 33747
Npsouthside937@gmail.com

James A. Neal is an urban fiction author with outstanding writing skills that will have you turning page after page. He is from St. Petersburg, Florida, back with another hood banger, GMC Get Money Clique 2. Since his release from state prison, he hasn't looked back. Dropping his first book July/23/2018, he really has something to prove. After losing both of his parents while incarcerated he said that he would do it for them!